RICHARD STEELE

PRIVATE EYE

SOLID STEELE ALIBI

David C. Reyes

New Harbor Press

New Harbor Press
1601 Mt Rushmore Rd, Ste 3288
Rapid City, SD 57701
www.newharborpress.com

Ordering Information:
Quantity sales. Special discounts are available on quantity purchases by corporations, associations, and others. For details, contact the "Special Sales Department" at the address above.

Richard Steele - Private Eye/Reyes —1st ed.

ISBN 978-1-63357-412-0

First edition: 10 9 8 7 6 5 4 3 2 1

Contents

Chapter One

The contrast of the lighted window illuminated his office against the dark of the night. Steele was up late working on a case in his office, as usual. It was around 9 pm on a Friday, and rest assured, he would be there until after midnight. Steele couldn't sleep during this time of night—his memories wouldn't let him. Thoughts cascaded in his mind to that fateful night. The night that took his world away.

Steele closed the file which lay on his mahogany pedestal desk. The file represented a case of an upscale debutant who lost her cocker spaniel. The woman was so involved in her lush upscale life, that she failed to realize the side yard gate was left open by the gardener. Snookie, as she called her, had apparently got out and was making time with a Boston terrier down the street when Steele found the dog. Perhaps a litter of Boston-spaniel puppies was on the way. Only time and a rounded belly would tell.

As he thought about the case, Steele frowned with irony and shook his head. His PI business had started with a bang of an insurance fraud investigation and a government coverup. But within the past year, his recent cases were literally going to the dogs. Steele wanted more; more adventure, more intrigue. He needed something or someone who would rattle the cage of mediocrity of stale investigations since he began his PI business over two years ago.

Surely, he thought, *business should start to pick up now that we're in 1947; two years after the war.*

As he sat pondering these things, Steele's ears caught the sound of a saxophone filtering up from the jazz club directly below his office. As the crescendo of the note began to trail off, his ears perked up to the sound of footsteps. Similar to the pitter-patter of a gazelle walking along a riverbed, any red-blooded American male knew that sound like they knew the back of their hand. It was the sound of a woman's high heels steadily making their way up the steps to his office.

Steele reopened the dog-eared case as to appear busy at his desk. *You never want to appear desperate for a case. It leaves too much room in negotiating your price.*

Steele sat in his weathered Gunlocke chair with his shoes propped up upon his desk, with the file in hand. The patter on the steps reached the top of the stairs, as the silhouette of a shapely woman filtered through the frosted glass of the door. As the creak of the rusted hinges swung open, Steele glanced up from the pages of the open file. A striking woman with golden blonde hair stepped confidently through the door and looked around as if she owned the joint. With a pink Victory business suit that pleated and flared at the knee and a white Fedora hat; this dame, he thought, was dressed to kill.

The woman stood with a stone-cold look pasted across her face and glared at Steele. Like a predator cat debating whether or not to pounce on its prey, she took a few steps forward toward his desk.

Steele looked her over; noting every curve. *This doll face has more sex appeal than should be legally allowed.*

Steele held that famous thin-lipped smile of his. Most people never knew if that smile meant he was reserving comment, or that he knew something which they didn't.

Her eyes looked him over. "Richard Steele, I presume?" Her voice was swarthy but feminine.

"Yes, I'm Steele." He looked her over. "And I'm sure you presume a lot more than just my name."

The woman caught his remark with the slight raise of her sculptured cheekbones, then they slipped back into place.

"I heard that about you," she said with a blank stare.

Steele leaned back in his chair and laced his fingers on the back of his head. "You heard what about me? People say a lot of things about me; both good and bad."

Her eyes looked him over. "Well let me start with the good. People are right when they say you're very handsome and look a lot like Cary Grant. I would throw in Tyrone Power, but with more rugged features." Her eyes glanced him over once more. "Not that your looks impress me, mind you; it's just my observation. However, they also say you can charm any woman with a smile from one side of your mouth, then bite them like a viper from the other."

Steele half laughed, revealing that charming smile. "And which one of those two women might you be?"

The woman raised one eyebrow. "Neither, because I'm not *any woman*."

Steele acknowledged her smooth play with a crack of a smile. "So, doll face; you appear to know a lot about me, but I know nothing about you. Why don't we start with your name?"

She pointed to the chair in front of his desk. "May I?"

Steele lowered his hand in presenting fashion. "Sure, take a load off."

She glanced at the chair; almost as if she found it repellant.

"What's the matter," he said. "It's not going to bite."

The woman reached into her purse and pulled out a handkerchief and dusted off the chair. "It looks rather dusty. Haven't had many clients lately?" she said with sarcasm.

Steele lowered his feet off the desk and pointed to the file. "As far as clients, I was just finishing up a case right now."

The woman took a seat and crossed her long shapely legs. "One observation is I can tell you are a bonified gumshoe."

"And how do you know that?"

"Your shoes. When I first came in, you had your feet up on your desk. I saw your Oxford shoes with rubber soles were worn out. Not to mention, you have a piece of chewing gun on one of them. You might want to think about a new pair."

Steele held her gaze. "Very good, you are a very observant woman. But I have to warn you, I'm very observant too."

"That's good because that is why I'm here. I need someone who is on the ball and doesn't let anything get past him." She placed the handkerchief back in her purse. "My name is Evette Hamilton. But I prefer to be called Eve."

"Eve, huh? The mother of all living; or so I heard growing up in Sunday school."

Her eyes reflected a glimmer of surprise. "I didn't take you for a choir boy."

He reached into his desk and pulled out a pack of cigarettes. "No, no choir boy here," he said, then smacked the pack on the edge of the table. "My mother, God rest her soul, took me to church when I was a young boy and taught me a few things from the good book."

She glanced at the cigarettes. "May I have one—I'm no choir girl either," she said, in a revealing tone. She added, "I also like my drink."

Steele glanced at the bottle of bourbon sitting on the top shelf on his bookcase—unopened.

"Cigarettes are my vice," he said and took his cigarette lighter out of his pant pocket. He glanced once more at the bottle of bourbon. "And as far as drinking, I don't touch the hard stuff anymore."

She glanced at the bookcase. "Then why the bottle of bourbon?"

"As a reminder, not to touch the hard stuff anymore."

Her eyes narrowed in studying fashion. She was interested in the story behind that bottle, but now was not the time to discuss that.

Steele rose from his chair and walked around the desk and lay his leg across its edge. He leaned forward and extended the lighter. Eve leaned in with the cigarette in hand just enough to allow Steele a glimpse of her ample cleavage.

She took notice. "Like what you see?"

Steele withdrew the lighter, lifted his leg off the desk, and sat back down in his chair.

"What I see, is someone who has an angle. So, what's your game anyway?"

She took a puff of her cigarette. "So, you think I'm here to con you?"

He glanced at her from head to toe. "Among other things."

She shifted in the chair and crossed her legs once more. "Good, I like a man who's direct and says what he means. Even if he is making assumptions about me."

Steele casually puffed a breath of smoke. Then the tone of his voice changed; indicating he was ready to stop this play on words and get down to business.

"So, what can I do for you, Miss Hamilton?"

She held a stoic expression. "It's not Miss, it's Mrs. My husband is Randall Hamilton. You might have heard of his law firm—Randall Hamilton and Associates."

Steele nodded his head, then dabbed some ash in the tray. "I've heard of it; on Main Street downtown."

"Yes, I came here to acquire your services because I believe my husband may be having an affair."

Steele studied her eyes. "And why do you believe that?"

"Lately he seems to be distant from me and he is always working late. He also takes sudden unplanned trips out of town."

"Isn't working late and taking trips out of town par for the course for an attorney?"

"Yes, but it's more than just that. At times when he comes home, I can smell women's perfume on his clothes. Also, it seems lately he is not interested in, well let's just say, in showing me nightly affection."

Steele held an inquisitive smile. "Why, Mrs. Hamilton, are you blushing?"

She opened her purse, took out a compact, and powdered her nose. "Look, I may be a woman-about-town, but some subjects are best left behind closed doors." She then closed her compact with a snap of the lid.

Steele tapped some ash into the tray. "Fair enough; go on."

"Well, there are several women who are close to him because of his business. One of them being his..."

Steele held up his hand. "Look, before you start giving me details, I think we need to discuss my price."

She nodded in agreement. "Very well, name your price. I'll let you know if I feel your fees match your reputation and are worth my time."

Steele nodded his head with a slight grin. "I see... And I'll let you know if I think my time in dealing with a difficult dame like you, is worth *my time*."

She flippantly tossed her fingers in the air. "Touché, Mr. Steele. So, what are your fees?"

"I make $14 a day, plus expenses. With three days' wages in advance."

"Matt Stone charges $16 a day. Why are you so much less? Could it be he feels his time is worth more than yours?"

Steele huffed a half-laugh. "Look, we can sit here and play these games all day long. The difference is that Matt Stone blows his money on women and drinks his dinner from a bottle. I myself like to stay sharp, that way I know when someone's trying to con me."

"So, are we back to you not trusting me?"

"Look, it's not a matter of trust. It's the fact that I don't know anything about you—yet. But if you keep up this charade, I may have to charge you double my normal price."

Her cheekbones lifted with a sly smile. "Well, if it comes to that, I'll just make sure the time you put into this investigation is doubly worth it."

Steele took out a notepad and licked the tip of the pencil. "Fine, let's start from the beginning; and don't leave anything out."

Eve Hamilton sat up straighter and folded her arms around her purse. "Before we get into these *other women*, I should start with my life at home. Randall and I first met at the governor's ball. He was so handsome in his double-breasted suit which took my breath away. We began courting in a whirlwind romance and before I knew it, we had fallen in love. However, the minute I mentioned marriage, I noticed a slight change in his demeanor. I couldn't put my finger on it, but it was as if he became guarded somehow. I didn't press him about it, and soon he proposed to me at his vacation home in Southport. One thing I want to mention is he sat me down about two weeks before the wedding. He placed a folder in front of me and when I opened it, it was a pre-nuptial agreement. I was a little taken back by it, but he went on to explain that it was to cover his business assets. He told me not to worry my pretty little head about it, that it was just a formality. At the time I didn't think too much about it and went ahead and signed it. Later, I had an attorney look it over. It basically said that all monies and assets acquired prior to our marriage were his, and I would not be entitled to any of it. Any monies acquired jointly after our marriage, I would receive fifty percent if there was a dissolution of marriage, or upon his death. For the first few years, everything seemed fine. But soon he started to become possessive of anything I did and especially bought. It was like he placed a leash on me, and he gave me a monthly allowance for my spending. I mean, imagine that; placing an allowance on me is like placing a clunky western saddle on a thoroughbred. I need the freedom to live and breathe, not be strapped down like an old mare. This went on for a few months and when I couldn't take it anymore, I confronted him. I told him I needed a free hand when it came to my spending, and he had no right to treat me that way. He walked to the window which overlooks our front garden. Then he turned to me and said, 'There are things you don't know about my upbringing which have a bearing on my financial outlook on life. However, I feel your spending is out of control. In the beginning, I let you spend what you wanted, but you proved to me you lacked self-control. That's why I put you on a certain budget so you would learn about not overspending. I give you more money in one month than the average person would spend in six months. I'm sorry, but considering all factors, this is my money and I will not allow you to have a free hand in your spending. Until you can prove to me otherwise, this is the way it has to be—my word is final.' When I heard him make that ultimatum, that was the final straw. I made up my mind right then I was going to file for divorce when the time was right. But when I started to feel he was having an affair, I decided to wait to get proof of his infidelity. That way I would have a better case when we go to court over his assets and my alimony. I want more than just half of what he has earned since we got married—I deserve more."

Eve Hamilton glanced at the wall clock then cupped her hand to her mouth in a yawn.

Steele looked at the clock as well. "Maybe we should continue this tomorrow. Seems like you're a little tired."

Eve acknowledged with a nod. "Yes, perhaps you're right. My husband is away on a business trip right now, hence the reason I came here tonight. But perhaps we should continue tomorrow."

Steele stood to his feet. "I'll tell you what; why don't you write out some notes on all the women you want me to look into and then come back tomorrow. We can go over the list then. Make sure to note when and where they are together. For example; does she work with him, or does she work at a restaurant he frequents? Also, make a list of any locations and addresses where you feel they may be getting together. We'll fill in the blanks tomorrow."

Eve Hamilton rose from the chair. "Sounds good; I shall return tomorrow around 10:00 am. Oh, for the time being, do not attempt to call me. I don't want Randall to get suspicious."

"No, I won't. We'll figure something out later as far as communicating. And tomorrow morning if for some reason I'm running late, Kit will be here."

"And who is that?"

"Kit is my secretary assistant and very good friend to me."

Eve raised her brow. "A very good *woman friend*?"

Steele waved her off. "No, not like that. Kit is fifteen years old—I'm not a cradle robber."

Eve took a few steps towards the door. "Good night, Mr. Steele, I shall see you tomorrow."

Steele held his thin-lipped smile. "I'll be here."

As Mrs. Hamilton closed the door, Steele watched her silhouette fade out of view through the frosted glass. He smothered what was left of his cigarette into the tray and sat back in his chair. Earlier in the evening, Steele had said he wanted more; more adventure, more intrigue. However, after this first encounter with the provocative and intriguing Eve Hamilton, he realized he might be in for just that, and maybe more. However, there was something brewing in that famous gut of his, and he wondered if this case was going to be, as they say, a proverbial hornet's nest.

Chapter Two

Steele arrived back at his office at 6:00 am the next morning with his usual five hours of sleep. He opened the shades to the window facing the street and noted that a bright sunny day was ahead on this June morning. An hour later, Kit arrived in her trademark high-waisted jeans cuffed at the bottom, a short sleeve top, covered with a light jacket. As such, Kit wouldn't be caught dead in a poodle skirt like the other girls her age wore.

She waved hello, and walked towards the coat rack as her light brown hair in pigtails swayed back and forth. Inquisitive as she is, she raised her nose and took in a few sniffs of the air.

"Hey, was there someone in here last night? Namely a woman?"

Steele nodded his head. "Very good. Someday you'll be taking over my PI business with that sharp sense you have. Why don't you place your sack lunch in the refrigerator and take a seat? Before I go out to get some breakfast from the café, I'll fill you in on what happened last night."

Kit placed her lunch in the refrigerator and took a seat on the chair in front of his desk.

She leaned forward with interest. "So, do we have another case? I certainly hope so because lately, things have been pretty stale around here, and I'm not talking about the moldy cheese in the refrigerator."

Steele nodded his head. "Yeah, I know; I need to throw that cheese out. But at least we have a refrigerator and not an icebox. Otherwise, part of your duties would be to haul some ice blocks in from the local market."

"Why would I be the one to haul ice? You're a grown man and I'm just a teenager, and a girl to boot!"

Steele smiled. "Yes, you may be a girl, but you're probably stronger than most of the boys your age. Hey speaking of boys, I think Jake Meyers is sweet on you."

Kit's cheeks began to blush. "No he's not!" she retorted, then fidgeted in her seat. "Why would you say something like that?"

"Because we only pay for the Saturday edition of the Gazette. But lately, he's been coming in the afternoons when you are here, where 'he claims' he has extra weekday editions. Haven't you noticed?"

Kit pressed her lips together to suppress the grin lifting the edges of her lips.

"Just because he has extra papers doesn't mean nothing! Besides, why would he be sweet on me after we've known each other for years?"

Steele circled her face with his eyes. "Have you looked in a mirror lately, young lady? You may not see it, but you're starting to blossom into a pretty young woman."

Her eyes sparkled with interest. "You really think so? You're not just saying that to be nice, are ya? Because if you are teasing me, I may have to just haul off and slug you!"

Steele laughed. "You know Kit, that Tomboy attitude isn't going to keep the interest from the boys around here, like Jake. That moxie of yours is great out on the streets, but it's bupkis if you're trying to bag yourself a young man."

Kit crossed her arms. "First of all, I'm only fifteen and I'm not trying to 'bag' anything. And I'm not going to act like those prissy high school girls and their poodle skirts. No sir, not me; I ain't changing for nobody!"

Steele smiled, then looked towards the clock on the wall. "We can talk about your coming-of-age another time. Right now, I need to give you a few instructions before our client gets here. First of all, her name is Eve Hamilton. Her husband has a law firm downtown called Randall Hamilton and Associates. I believe it's in that five-story building on Main Street."

Kit grabbed a pad of paper and a pencil. "Should I be writing this down?"

Steele nodded. "Yes, you probably should. To cut to the chase, she thinks her husband may be having an affair. We will be investigating to see if we can catch him in the act. When Mrs. Hamilton gets here, she is supposed to have a list of the women she suspects her husband may be cheating with. When I get back from the café, I'll be going over that list with her to fill in the blanks. Now, when she gets here, I want you to be on your guard."

Kit drew an inquisitive stare. "Why? Be on my guard for what?"

"This dame has something up her sleeve—I just feel it. She's very sharp and I feel she has some kind of motive besides looking into her husband. For example, one minute she was being flirtatious with me, so I assumed she was single. Then the next minute, her face turns stone cold and she tells me she's married. She's a hard one to figure out. Also, she may try to ask you some questions about me or my past. Be careful what you tell her. Don't tell her too much, just the basics. She doesn't need to know about what happened in Rachel's death."

Kit lowered her gaze recalling what she knew about Steele's late wife Rachel. She then lifted her eyes to meet his. "I understand, I'll be careful."

"Now I also want you to do something for me. Mrs. Hamilton mentioned that lately, her husband started to put her on a spending allowance. It seemed to be a sore spot with her, so try to draw that out. She might let something slip with you, whereas she might be more guarded with me. I felt there was more to that part of her life than she was leading on. You can tell me about it later."

"I will. I'll find an opening and casually bring something up on that subject."

Steele walked over to the coat rack and took hold of his tan trench coat. "I'll be back in a little while. Do you want me to bring you something?"

"Sure, can you get me a clodhopper and a chocolate milk?"

Steele lowered his brow. "A clodhopper?"

"Yeah, that's what we used to call them at this one foster home. I think the café calls them bear-claws."

Steele smiled and nodded. "Okay, I'll get one for you."

Steele walked down the steps from his office and panned the street which was just coming to life. The Victorian light posts which lined the street and rising sun were a familiar sight on his walk to the café.

Westend Café was a landmark in the city, and Steele had a routine of going there often for breakfast. Monday morning's special of the day was steak and eggs and breakfast potatoes. A far cry better than the Spam and oatmeal from a few years earlier due to rationing from the war.

Steele walked into the café and greeted the waitress with a wave. Betsy acknowledged him with a friendly wave in return and a broad smile. She had worked there for the past five years and had the perfect disposition for the job. Steele always thought she might have a little crush on him being a handsome man, but being her job, she kept it professional.

Betsy walked up to the table with a carafe in her hand. "Hello Mr. Steele; how are you this morning?" She then turned his cup upright and poured in some coffee.

"Fine Betsy; and you?"

"I'm doing very well, thank you. So, will it be the special today?"

Steele smiled. "Yep, you know me so well. I'll take the steak medium-well and my eggs over-easy."

Betsy smiled. "I'll get that up in a jiffy. Anything else?"

"Yes, besides the usual box of assorted donuts, can you bag up a bear-claw and a carton of chocolate milk for Kit? And can you put everything on my tab?"

She nodded. "No problem."

Steele rose from the table and walked over to the register and tossed a nickel in the jar and took hold of the New York Times newspaper. He liked to keep an eye on the Blue Jays, a minor league team in Charlotte, and of course the Yankees. He opened the newspaper and perused the different headlines as the scent of the freshly brewed coffee filtered up from his steaming cup.

Betsy then brought the box of a dozen donuts and placed them on the table.

"It's so nice that you help those homeless people out at The Alley on 42nd Street," she said, referring to the donuts. "You have a caring heart, Mr. Steele."

"Thank you for saying that, Betsy. I have a lot to be thankful for."

Steele then looked out the window in remembrance. It wasn't too long ago when *he himself* called The Alley his home. As he waited for his breakfast, he continued to read different articles when a particular advertisement caught his eye. It read; {Randall Hamilton and Associates for all your legal needs.} In turn, Steele thought about the upcoming case with Eve Hamilton. Unlike most of his cases involving a cheating spouse, this one seemed to cause him to take in a breath of anxiety. This was uncommon for Steele's usual calm, collected demeanor.

Betsy brought over his breakfast plate and set it down. "Anything else?"

Steele looked over the food and smiled. "No, it looks really good, thank you. But why don't you add another donut to my tab so you can have one on your break."

Betsy waved him off. "No, I appreciated you doing that for me from time to time, but just last week my boss told me not to accept anything from the customers. He said something about keeping a professional distance."

Steele shook his head and rolled his eyes. "Professional distance? Seems like after the war being neighborly has come under suspicion. I hope friendly conversations with the customers won't go the way of the Dodo bird."

"No, my boss wants us to be friendly so our customers will return and give good tips. He used the term, friendly but professional."

Steele proceeded to eat his breakfast while watching the city street come to life. Stan the flower man, a street-side vendor who sold his flowers from a cart, began setting things up. Chrysanthemums were the special of the day—.25 cents a dozen.

Steele finished his meal then left a generous tip for Betsy as he took hold of the box of donuts. He then walked over to his 39' Chevy Fleet Line and placed the donuts in the passenger seat and got on his way.

At the corner of 42nd and Milner was an alleyway—hence the name, The Alley. A group of homeless people called this alleyway their home. Occupants ranged anywhere from seven to twelve in number at any given time. When Steele was there, he knew about nine regulars.

Steele took hold of the box of donuts and got out of his car. As he made his way down the alley, you could see several heads perk up at his arrival. Like a group of hound dogs lifting their heads at the sound of a whippoorwill, they turned their heads to acknowledge Steele approaching. But even though he had regularly brought them something to eat for the past two years, there was no expectation on their part. Disappointment was a part of their lives—they assumed nothing.

Steele walked up and approached a man named John. Most people who lived on the streets only went by their first or last name, but never both.

He greeted with a wave. "Hey John, how are you this morning?"

John sat up straighter while sitting on an old mattress. "Morning, Richard, it's always good to see you." He glanced at the box of donuts. "And I'm not just talking about the goodies in your hand. When you lived here for a time, I used to enjoy our talks."

"Me too. Any luck in finding some work?"

John shrugged his shoulders. "I've done a few odds and ends, but nothing steady. It's only been a couple of years since the war, so the economy is still slow."

Steele patted his shoulder. "Well hang in there; things are starting to pick up. I would hire you to do some of the cleanup and maintenance at my office, but as you know I have Kit working for me. That girl works like her tails on fire."

Steele opened the box of donuts for John to choose his preference.

He took hold of the donut with a look of appreciation. "Thanks, Richard, it's so rare that a former occupant ever returns here to visit, much less helps us out. You're a good man."

"Well, I don't know if I'm such a good man, as much as I feel that I'm a blessed man. I'm just trying to pay back what was given to me when Kit helped me get back on my feet."

John took a bite of the donut and nodded his head. "Say hello to her for me."

Steele nodded. "I will."

He proceeded to hand out donuts to the rest of the homeless. The ones he knew, he spent a few minutes talking with them, as the others conveyed their appreciation with a simple, thank you.

Meanwhile, Kit was busy doing cleanup chores when she heard footsteps walking up the stairs. She waited with a broom in hand, as a woman walked in the door. The woman was dressed in a high-end business suit.

"Hello," Kit greeted. "How can I help you?"

The woman scanned Kit up and down. "I am Eve Hamilton. I have an appointment with Mr. Steele. You must be Kat."

Kit noted she said her name wrong but said nothing about it. She began to walk towards Mrs. Hamilton to shake her hand when suddenly, she stopped midstride. She realized her hands must be dirty from the sweeping.

"I'm sorry," she said apologetically. "I would shake your hand but my hands are pretty dirty.

Eve Hamilton lowered her eyes to take a look at Kit's hands but said nothing else.

"So," Eve said, glancing around the room. "When will Mr. Steele be in the office?"

Kit walked to the closet and placed the broom inside. "He should be back anytime. He went to the café for breakfast, then he had a few errands to run." Kit pointed to the chair. "Have a seat while you wait."

Eve Hamilton walked over and elegantly took a seat, then rested her handbag against one of the chair legs.

She looked Kit over. "What exactly do you do for Mr. Steele?"

Kit perked up, as she was very proud of her role in their relationship.

"I work part-time; a few hours in the morning and a few in the afternoon as his girl-Friday. Plus I work full time with him on the weekends and during summer vacation. I type investigation notes and manage the cases in the file cabinets. I also run different errands for Rick; like shopping for supplies for the office and do clean-up chores. I'm also here as a sounding board when we're working on a case." Kit hesitated. She remembered what Steele had said about saying too much in front of Mrs. Hamilton.

She continued. "I'm mean, it's not like I'm his partner or anything, Rick is the one who does most of the investigation; I just help out a little."

A pondering stare rose upon Eve Hamilton's face. "Tell me, Kat; you must be very close to Mr. Steele seeing how you call him Rick."

"Well, we've known each other for the past four years, so yeah, I call him Rick. But when we are at some city office or some professional place, then I call him Mr. Steele."

"And where did you two first meet? For example, I understand that he used to be a police investigator."

Kit thought to be careful how she answered. "Well, that's kind of a long story of how we met. Some of the details I'll let Rick tell you if he wants. In short, after Rick's wife died, his life kind of fell apart. Things went bad with his job and soon he was let go from the police department. I met Rick when he was in a bad place and drinking a lot. I had grown up in many foster homes and some were not good circumstances, so I would take to the streets to get away for a while. I guess you could say I understood him better than most. When we first met and started talking, we seemed to get along really well. He told me that my brash attitude and advice of picking himself off the floor woke him up. From there he sobered up and began to turn his life around to the point he started this private investigator business. He brought me along with him and we've been together ever since."

Eve Hamilton directed a penetrating stare. It was as if she was studying Kit for what she *didn't say*, rather than what *she did* say.

She then cleared her throat. "Tell me, Kat, you mentioned that Mr. Steele used to be a drunk?"

"I didn't say that!" she snapped. "And the name is Kit, not Kat! All I meant was he needed to stop drinking because it was affecting his life."

"Sorry about the name but I thought Mr. Steele had called you Kat, which is usually short for Katherine. What is Kit short for?"

Kit glanced to the side somberly in remembrance, then return eye contact.

"I don't know for sure because I was only five years old. All I remember is that my parents used to call me Kit before they died. However, when I was placed into a foster home, there were some official papers from the orphanage that said my full name was

Kittridge Lawson. Maybe they got that off of some birth papers they found when they cleaned out my parents' house. I had an aunt that lived in St. Louis, but she died a few years before my parents."

"Sorry to hear about your parents," Eve said, as a matter of fact. She then glanced at the bottle on the shelf. "So, tell me about that bottle of bourbon. Mr. Steele mentioned to me it was a reminder to him not to drink. What happened that was so awful that would change a man from a respected police officer to being a heavy drinker?"

Kit stiffened with caution. She decided to turn this conversation in her favor.

"Why are you so concerned about Rick's drinking habits of his past? By all these personal questions about him, sounds like you are interested in him in a romantic way. He's very handsome, so there are a lot of women that find him attractive."

Eve Hamilton sat up straighter with slight annoyance. "I'll have you know that I am a married woman. And even though I think my husband may be cheating on me, that doesn't mean I'll be throwing myself at another man anytime soon. I just want to make sure Mr. Steele is the type of man with integrity given his past problems with drinking. I want to make sure I get my money's worth in this investigation."

Kit's eyes sparkled, as this opened the door for her. "Your money's worth? Rick is definitely worth every cent. But tell me," Kit said and glanced at Eve's outfit. "Why are you so concerned about getting your money's worth? You seem to have a lot of money by the way you dress."

Kit's statement struck a chord. Eve then took on an indignant tone in her voice.

"My husband may be a successful lawyer, but that doesn't mean I have carte blanche on buying everything I want or deserve. My husband is stingy and gives me a weekly allowance for spending. So yes, I have to watch what I spend as this investigation is coming out of my spending allowance." Eve glanced out the corner of her eye, then added. "Hopefully soon, I won't ever have to be on an allowance again. A woman of my breeding and class should never be treated that way." She cleared her throat. "Anyway, to answer your question, that is why I'm concerned about how I spend my money in hiring Mr. Steele."

Kit's ears perked up and turned towards the front door. "I think that's Rick coming up the stairs."

Steele opened the door with a bag and a carton of chocolate milk from the café.

"Hello Mrs. Hamilton," he said and handed Kit the donut bag and the milk. "I see you are right on time. Sorry, I'm a little late but I had an errand to take care of."

Kit motioned her hand towards the file room. "I'll be eating my donut and doing some filing. I'll shut the door to give you some privacy."

He nodded in acknowledgment. "Thanks, Kit."

She shut the door as Steele took a seat at his desk. As his eyes looked Eve over, a sense of caution rushed over him. Something told him this was going to be a humdinger of an investigation with many twists and turns. But Steele needed the money—there were bills to pay.

He glanced at the notebook in her hands. "Is that the list of possible suspects whom your husband may be cheating with?"

"Yes, I will read you the notes I have on each one. I'll begin with the woman I suspect the least, to the one I suspect the most."

Steele took out a notebook along with a pencil. "Okay, go ahead."

"The first one on my list is my husband's secretary. Her name is May Wilson. Miss Wilson has worked for my husband for about three years. She works side by side with him for hours at a time. I know that's her job, but I can tell my husband is very fond of her. At times when he is talking about his job, he always seems to bring her up in a complementary way. When I have casually brought up the subject spending time with her outside the office, he says their lunches are business-related, but I'm not so sure I believe that."

Steele interjected. "Do you know where they might go to lunch? For example, do you have a list of particular restaurants or cafés?"

"Yes, I know he goes with her to The Towner Steakhouse which is downtown. Also, the Yorkshire Café in the midtown area."

"And do you know where Miss Wilson lives, and if she lives alone? I ask, because if she lives fairly close to his work, they may be having their rendezvous at her place."

"Yes, she lives alone and she lives in the suburbs in Arlington. I can get you the exact address and call you with that information."

Steele took notes to all that Eve said on the first suspect. She seemed very genuine as she provided the information. Unlike the cat and mouse antics she displayed in their first meeting.

Eve read the next one on the list. "The next woman I suspect is Darlene Thomas. She is the customer relations manager at the Lakeside Golf & Country Club which we are members of. Whenever I have gone to the club to see him, many times I have seen them talking together. I also noted the perfume she wears when I have spoken to her. Sometimes, when my husband gets home, he smells like this perfume."

Steele interrupted. "Have you noted Miss Wilson's perfume? I'm asking because it could be the same brand as Darlene Thomas."

"I haven't noticed, but I rarely go to his office so there is a possibility she wears the same kind—good point."

Steele licked the tip of his pencil. "Getting back to Miss Thomas, do you know where she lives, or a place they may secretly have their rendezvous?"

"Yes, but she lives in a modest apartment complex, so I doubt my husband would use her place for his affair. However, I can get you into the country club to be able to spy on her. If she is the one, he might make plans to get together with her while he is there at the club."

Steele gathered a thought. "Oh, I almost forgot; what do these women look like? I need a description for all of them."

"Yes, I supposed that would be helpful. The first woman, May Wilson, has light brown hair with a nice figure and very pretty. She is about five-foot-four and is usually wearing a business suit or some other office attire. She usually wears rose-colored lipstick—nothing too ostentatious. Next, Darlene Thomas has dark brown hair with very pretty big eyes. Because of her job, she usually wears a club uniform of navy dress pants and a white blouse. She is about my height which is five-foot-seven. Now, the last woman on my list, and the one I suspect the most, is Poppy Sorenson. And just like her name, she has a very bright and bubbly personality. She has strawberry blonde hair and a figure that just won't quit. And as you can tell," she said and glanced down at her own figure, "My husband has a type he likes. Anyway, Poppy owns a property management business in Southport where my husband owns a vacation home. She takes care of all aspects of property management; like handling the gate security company, landscape maintenance, house cleaning, and she prepares the house when he is having a gathering. We spend two weeks there in the summer, along with various weekend trips. However, my husband goes there a lot on what he calls, 'business-related weekends.' During these weekends, he prefers I do not go with him. He says he's very busy and he would rather I stay at home or I'll be bored. Usually, on those weekends he gives me extra money to go shopping or to spend time with my friends. However, it seems like every time I call him when he's there in Southport, Poppy always *just happens* to be there. When I ask him why she's there, he claims it is for property management reasons. This is why I suspect her the most. Southport is three and a half hours away from our home here in Charlotte. Since it is so far away, he knows I would not be able to just show up and catch him with her."

Steele continued to write his notes. "And do you know in advance when your husband and this Poppy will be at the vacation house? Being so far away, I will have to book a motel nearby and stay a couple of days as I investigate. Also, when I mentioned my price, booking a motel is considered an expense, so you would have to pay for that also."

"Actually, I will be going with you when you go out to Southport. That house is very large and has security gates to which only I, my husband, and Poppy have keys. Also, if he is having an affair, we need to catch him in the act. I know the house and landscape, so I will be able to show you the best way to get a photo of them together."

Steele held a questioning stare. "I know you want photos, but what if they break away from a romantic embrace before I can take photos of them? Won't we still have positive proof with us as witnesses?"

Eve Hamilton reached into her purse and pulled out her lipstick. "The photos are for the courts," she said and applied a shimmer to her lips. "My husband owns a law firm. He and his team of lawyers know all the ins and outs of beating a rap. When I take him to court, I need photos as proof. Then with you as a firsthand witness, that should be enough to prove my case." She added. "And by the way, I do not stay in *motels*," she said, in a snobbish tone. "We will stay in an upscale hotel—I have certain standards."

Steele shook his head. "Well *excuse me*..." he glanced down at his clothes. "Is my current attire going to be a problem for this 'upscale' hotel of yours?" he said with sarcasm.

Eve scanned his clothes from head to toe. "Well, I presume you own a suit, don't you? Some of the restaurants we will be going to require a tie. You do have one of those, don't you?"

Steele gritted his teeth in irritation but kept his cool. "Yes, I do have a tie. Now, I presume I will have my own hotel room?"

Eve's eyes grew wide with indignance. "Of course you will have your own room! What kind of a woman do you think I am?"

Steele held a blank expression while he wrote more notes. However, inside he was smiling. He threw out that question about separate rooms to see her reaction to her own fidelity.

"Alright, I think I got the picture. I will be starting with the first woman on your list; his secretary Miss Wilson." Steele rose to his feet. "Would there be anything else?"

Eve glanced at the bottle of bourbon sitting on the bookshelf. "Someday, I want you to tell me about that bottle. Kit mentioned something in brief about it, but I would like to know the full story."

Steele looked over to the bottle then back to Eve. "Maybe someday. If I find there comes a time when I feel my telling you that story will not jeopardize anything, then yes, I might tell you about that."

Eve rose to her feet. "Very well, Mr. Steele; I will be going."

He glanced at her purse. "Aren't you forgetting something?"

An inquisitive look rose on her face. "Forgetting something? What are you referring to?"

Steele held out an open hand. "My payment? I told you I get three days' wages in advance."

A look of recollection drew upon her face. "I'm sorry, I do remember you saying that."

She took hold of her purse and pulled out an inner pocketbook. She withdrew a large sum of cash and counted out the money on his desk.

"Here are forty-five dollars," she said and began to walk towards the door. She glanced back. "I do know that fourteen times three is forty-two. I threw in the extra for good measure. Oh, by the way, don't spend all of that in one place."

Steele glanced at the money on his desk. "Don't worry about me," he said with a sly smile. "I always spend my money wisely—very wisely."

Chapter Three

The next day Steele got right to work. Whenever he was working on a case, it became his priority until he saw it to its conclusion.

He sat at his desk writing out a plan on how he was going to approach the first person on the list—Miss May Wilson. Kit would not be in today as she was called in to cover for someone at the grocery store. Steele always appreciated Kit's feedback when he wrote out his investigative plan. She had a down-to-earth street-wise approach to things, which always worked well with Steele's methodical method.

Steele knew he needed a way to get in the door to Mr. Hamilton's law firm. As he tapped the pencil on his desk in rapid succession, his eyes grew large.

I got it! I will make an appointment with the law firm on how to legally set up a trust fund. I'll say I'm helping my sister as she is currently tied up enrolling her kids in a new school. This will get me in the door and I can scope things out with Miss Wilson first, and then with Mr. Hamilton himself. I'm usually good at reading people, so hopefully, I can pick up on the subtle nuances of both of them.

Steele searched the phone book for Hamilton Law Firm, then reached for the phone sitting on his desk and dialed the number. As he waited for it to be answered, he quickly thought of a pseudonym instead of his real name.

A woman's voice answered. "Hamilton and Associates, may I help you?"

"Yes, my name is Jeffrey Reid and I want to make an appointment with Mr. Hamilton regarding setting up a trust fund for my sister's children."

"Will your sister be joining you at the appointment?"

"No, unfortunately she is tied up right now. She just moved to Raleigh and she is busy with moving into her new house and trying to get her kids enrolled in school."

"Very well. However, at some point, we are going to need her signature on the trust documents. Also, Mr. Hamilton may not be the attorney who you will be dealing with at your introductory appointment. We have several attorneys here in this law firm."

"I see. But is there any way to get an appointment specifically with Mr. Hamilton? He came highly recommended to me, and that's why I chose this law firm in the first place."

"Well, let me see his appointments." Silence filled the line as she scanned the appointment book. Then she returned. "Okay, actually you are in luck. We had a cancellation for tomorrow at 10:00 am. Is that fine with you?"

"Yes, 10:00 am will be just fine. Is there anything I need to bring to the appointment?"

"Just basic information regarding your sister and her children. The ages of the children and how many funds each child will be allotted in the trust. For reoccurring deposits, we have a minimum amount of twenty dollars."

"No problem. I'll gather up that information and be there at 10:00 am sharp."

*****

Steele arrived at his office the next morning. He advised Kit of his plan of using the appointment to gather information for the case. He had a sister, but they were not very close. She was three years younger than him and did not have any children. Plus, she lived on the west coast in California. Steele told Kit to make sure she stayed in the office while he was gone. He wanted her to be there just in case Mrs. Hamilton was to call or stop by the office.

As Steele began to drive to the office building on Main Street, he took a deep breath to the forthcoming conversations with both Miss Wilson and Mr. Hamilton. He knew he needed to have his business face on.

He arrived at the location and parked in a side parking lot. As he walked towards the front of the building, he just hoped that no one would recognize him. He was listed in the phone book, but did not have his name on a billboard like Hamilton and Associates, nor did he advertise in the local newspaper, but he was still known to have his own business in town.

As he entered the double doors of the building, he walked over to the business directory and found Hamilton and Associates listed on the fifth floor, suite 501. A woman and her little girl boarded the elevator on the third floor. With the sight of the little girl, a thought suddenly entered his mind.

I almost forgot. I need to come up with fictitious names for my sister's children. He gathered a thought. *I know, I can use the names of the actors from the movie, It's a Wonderful Life. I'll call the kids Jimmy and Donna. Jimmy as in Jimmy Stewart, and Donna, as in Donna Reed. That should take care of the fictitious children.*

He got off on the fifth floor and walked over to suite 501 and entered the room.

The secretary sitting at the front desk greeted him with a smile. "May I help you?"

Steele glanced at her nameplate which read, May Wilson, then returned his focus.

"Yes, I'm Mr. Reid, Jeffrey Reid. I have an appointment with Mr. Hamilton at 10:00 am."

She glanced down at her appointment book. "Yes, Mr. Reid, please take a seat and he will be with you shortly. He is running a bit late from his prior appointment, but it shouldn't be too long."

Steele took a seat and held a smile on the inside. This was the perfect opportunity he needed to talk to Miss Wilson for his investigation. As he glanced across the room, he could understand why Eve might suspect the fetching Miss Wilson—she was definitely a looker.

He glanced her way once more. "Very fine morning, isn't it?"

"Yes," she said lifting her head. "It seems like it's going to be a warm day."

"So," he quickly added to keep her attention. "Have you worked for Mr. Hamilton very long?"

"Yes, three years and two months to be exact."

"And do you enjoy it? Is Mr. Hamilton a nice gent to work for?"

Miss Wilson glanced to the side as if recalling a particular event. "Oh yes, very much so. He is a true gentleman and treats me splendidly. He is an educated and accomplished man, but he never makes you feel inferior in any way."

"Is he a married man? If you don't mind me asking."

"Yes, he has a wife; her name is Eve. Mr. Hamilton rarely speaks of her so I don't know much about her. She doesn't come into the office very often, so I can't say I know her very well. And when she does come in, she says a brief hello, then goes straight into his office. She's quite pretty and carries herself in high regard."

Steele motioned with his hand in prodding fashion. "Meaning..."

Miss Wilson hesitated as if wanting to choose her words wisely. "Meaning, it's not my place to say considering I don't know her very well. But let's just say, she's a woman about town."

Steele nodded his head. "Yes, I understand—I know the type. And what about you? I would assume a pretty young woman like yourself is married?" he said with a bit of that Steele charm.

She smiled at his compliment. "No, I'm not married, nor at this stage in my life do I want to be."

Steele leaned forward with interest. "Why do you say that?"

"I like my life and my job. I also have other career pursuits, so I don't want anything to get in the way of that. I do want to find a nice man and get married someday; just not in the near future. Besides, some of the marriages I have seen, well let's just say, don't seem too happy after a few years."

Steele saw the opportunity so he forged forward. "Like Mr. and Mrs. Hamilton's marriage?"

She stared at him with caution. "Why are you asking me about their marriage? You're not a divorce attorney, are you?"

"Do they need a divorce attorney?" he countered, with a clever smile.

Miss Wilson turned her attention back to the file on her desk. "I don't feel it's my place to say, or do I want to continue with the direction of this conversation."

Steele held up an apologetic hand. "I'm sorry, I didn't mean to offend you. However, I do know what you're talking about. My sister, the one which I'm looking to set up that trust fund, is divorced herself. It's funny, but since the end of the war, I've seen a lot of women become more independent. Maybe because their role changed as they held down the home-front, and I suppose it filtered over to their home lives. Meaning, they don't put up with any abuse or cheating by their spouses anymore. In turn, the divorce rate has gone up." He added. "I read a lot of periodicals."

Miss Wilson glanced to the side but said nothing else.

Steele could tell the subject seemed to strike a chord with her. *Could she be the one who is having the affair with Mr. Hamilton? By some of her defensive reactions, it's definitely a possibility.*

A few minutes later, the door to Mr. Hamilton's office opened and his earlier appointment left out the front door.

He walked over and extended his hand. "I am Randall Hamilton."

Steele stood to his feet and shook his hand firmly. "I'm Rich..." suddenly he caught himself. He half-laughed. "Sorry, my middle name is Richard. I'm Jeff, Jeffrey Reid."

"Well, come into my office, Mr. Reid. We can discuss the possibilities of setting up that trust fund."

Steele took a seat across from Mr. Hamilton. Mr. Hamilton, who was dressed in a gray pinstriped suit, opened a drawer and pulled out a workup sheet.

"Tell me Mr. Reid; who is this trust fund going to be for, and what is the purpose?"

"Right now, I'm just trying to gather information for my sister. She has two kids, age ten and seven and she wants to set up a trust fund for both of them. She wants to make sure that her kids receive her monies and assets in the event of her death or incapacitation. She is a single mother and she doesn't want her ex-husband to try to take anything from the kids. In their divorce, her husband gave up all rights to the children. He wanted nothing to do with them and moved clear across the country. But my sister doesn't trust him if something were to happen to her."

Mr. Hamilton nodded in the affirmative. "That's an excellent reason to set up a trust fund. Now, do you happen to know if this trust will only be attached to her assets in the event of her death, or does she want ongoing deposits into these accounts? You see, there are many reasons for setting up these types of accounts. Some are domestic accounts; such as you are talking about. Others are to manage and control the spending of investments to protect beneficiaries from poor judgment and waste. They are also used to avoid court-supervised probate of trust assets and to protect trust assets from the beneficiaries' creditors."

Steele raised his brow. "Well, that was a lot to take in. This is a lot more complicated than I thought. Do you have some kind of pamphlet that I can take to her so she can look it over? Then once she has more time to deal with this, we can make another appointment with you."

Mr. Hamilton smiled. "Yes, it can get complicated, but when she comes in, I will break it down for her." He reached into a drawer. "Here is a pamphlet which will guide her to making the best choice."

Steele took hold of the pamphlet and placed it in his shirt pocket. He then glanced at a glass display case that sat at one end of his office.

"May I have a look?" he said, rising to his feet.

Mr. Hamilton turned to see what he was referring to. "You mean my gun display case?"

"Yes," he said and walked over to the case. He peered inside. "Is that an old Spencer Rifle? It looks Civil War era."

"Yes, it is," Mr. Hamilton said proudly. "It's a Spencer Repeating Carbine, dating back to 1862."

Steele moved closer and reached out to rest his hand on the glass case when Mr. Hamilton held him off.

"If you please, I am very particular of anyone touching that display. I know that might sound strange, but I was brought up in a very strict family. I have a bad habit of being very particular of everything needing to be in its place."

Steele moved his hand away from the case. "No, I understand. Something as valuable as this definitely should be kept protected."

"Well, it's more than just that. When I was growing up in my parent's house, we were very poor. And when the great depression hit, and with five in our family, things got very tough. I was nineteen when the depression started, and there were times when I went without food so my younger brothers and sisters could have enough to eat. I made an oath to myself that when the depression was over, I was going to get an education and never be poor again. So that's what I did. I went to law school and then started this law firm."

Steele thought on his statement. *I think I understand why Mr. Hamilton is careful with his money. It makes sense that he only gives his wife Eve a certain amount for spending. Taking care of his money is deeply seeded in him.*

Steele glanced at the gun case once more. "Is this the only vintage gun you own?"

Mr. Hamilton shook his head and smiled. "No, collecting guns is one of my vices. I own about fifteen other classic guns; including a Colt single-action revolver like Billy the Kid used."

Steele raised his brow in amazement. "That's quite the collection. Where do you keep the rest of your guns?"

"At my house in Southport. They are locked up in another gun case; a much bigger one than this. Then my guns are double-locked, as I always keep the door to my study locked with a Schlage deadbolt lock. Only I and my wife, Eve, have a key to that office." He gathered a thought. "Correction; my caretaker, Poppy, also has a key if I need her to get something out of the study when I'm here in Charlotte."

After he made that statement, Steele took note of his expression. It was as if there was more to the gun's story than he was letting on.

"You mentioned your wife. How long have the two of you been married?"

"About three years now. We met at a governor's ball."

"And do you have any children?"

"No, no children yet." He slightly frowned. "Given how my wife is, I'm not sure the pitter-patter of feet is in our near future. My wife is very particular about her figure. She sees what having children has done to her friends' figures and I don't think that appeals to her. My wife is a very strong-willed woman." He glanced at the clock on the wall. "I'm sorry, Mr. Reid but I have another appointment in another five minutes. Again, give that pamphlet to your sister, and if she is interested in moving forward, have her make an appointment with my secretary."

Steele thought quick to interject. "Yes, I met your secretary, Miss Wilson. She seems very nice and appears to be very competent—and very attractive."

Mr. Hamilton turned with an inquisitive stare. "Are you interested in my secretary, Mr. Reid?" The tone in his voice indicated slight displeasure in the thought.

"I was just making a statement," Steele replied. "I was just commenting on how nice she seems. I enjoyed my little talk with her."

Mr. Hamilton lowered his brow. "I see..." he said and studied Steele for a moment. He walked Steele to the door. "You take care, Mr. Reid. Perhaps one day we will run into each other again."

Steele held that thin-lipped smile. "Perhaps, Mr. Hamilton; perhaps."

Chapter Four

Steele arrived the next morning to find that Kit had arrived early also and was settling in.

"Morning Kit, how are you doing?"

"Good morning, Rick. It's nice to be able to come to work full time now that it's summer vacation. I wish I didn't have to go to school, that way I could work with you more than just a few hours in the mornings, and a couple after I get out of school."

"Speaking of work, how was your full day at work yesterday?"

Her cheeks lifted in a smile. "My day of work went pretty well. Mr. Timmons, the assistant store manager, said he can see me moving up to a cashier once I turn sixteen. Cashiers can't legally handle cash until they reach that age. It's some kind of a law, which I think is dumb because I can count cash with the best of them."

"Well, that day is just around the corner. Isn't your birthday in about a month?"

She smiled. "Yep, twenty-six days to be exact. Then I will be able to get my license to drive a car. Not that I have a car to drive, mind you, but still, I will be a legal adult."

"Not so fast there, missy. You're not considered to be a legal adult until you turn eighteen." He added with whimsy. "Then you can be drafted!"

"I can't be drafted; women don't get drafted. Besides, I've been out on my own anyway for so long, that it seems I'm an adult already."

Steele recalled Kit's life story of living at multiple foster homes and scrounging around on the streets for extra cash.

"Just don't try to grow up too soon. Enjoy your youth while you can. Once you're a true adult, that's when all the responsibility falls on you."

She nodded her head to his advice, then went to the broom closet and took hold of a rag and furniture polish.

As she began to polish the file cabinet, she glanced his way. "Say, what happened yesterday with your appointment to see Mr. Hamilton and his secretary?"

Steele unlocked the bottom drawer of his desk and took out the subject case file and opened it.

He scanned over his notes. "It went very well. I think I was able to get a little insight into both of them. First, I had a conversation with Miss Wilson who seems very nice and competent at her job. When I asked her questions about Mr. Hamilton, she seems to be genuinely fond of him as a person. I can't tell yet if that fondness is due to her being impressed by him, or if it's something else. When I casually asked her about Mr. Hamilton's wife, I gathered she was not particularly impressed by her. She didn't want to come out directly with her personal feelings, but the way she said that Mrs. Hamilton holds herself in 'high regard,' makes me feel she definitely has her opinions. I think she feels that Eve Hamilton thinks she's high-society and considers most people below her. Which honestly, matches my personal opinion of Eve Hamilton."

"And do you think she could be the one who is having the affair with Mr. Hamilton?"

Steele shrugged his shoulders. "I'm not sure at this point. I need more time to observe her and him together. Especially if I can see them outside of the office. That's where people let their hair down and show their true colors."

"And Mr. Hamilton; what did you find out about him?"

"For one, I'm actually impressed by him. And you know me, I'm not so easily impressed. He's an educated man and obviously wealthy, yet he doesn't act like he is higher class. I gathered he knows the ins and outs of being a lawyer. And if *he is* having an affair, it might not be so easy to catch him in the act. He seems very calculating, so I think he would be very discreet. He also appears to be one of those people who likes everything to be in its proper place. He has this vintage rifle in a display case. The case was so clean that there wasn't a single smudge mark on it. His entire office was very clean and immaculate."

"Did you cleverly work in the subject of Miss Wilson?"

"Yes, I did. He seems very fond of her; not only as his secretary but also as a person. I did provoke an interesting response from him. I made a statement that Miss Wilson was very attractive, which she is. That seemed to stir some emotion from him. He gave me this look like he was studying me, then asked me if I was interested in Miss Wilson. I played it off, but I felt there was a reason he asked me about her. I couldn't tell if his reaction is because he is having an affair with her, or he is just very protective of her. Either way, we need to investigate further when they are away from the office. I think I will have you get in contact with Eve Hamilton to have her call me or come by the office. Mr. Hamilton must have some kind of appointment book. I want Eve to find out when the next time he and Miss Wilson are going to a luncheon meeting so I can observe them."

"And how am I supposed to get in touch with Eve Hamilton when we are not to call her?"

Steele looked off in the distance thinking. Then a sneaky smile rose on his face.

"How do you think you would look in a Girl Scout uniform? We can pick up a used one at The Salvation Army."

Kit's eyes grew wide. "Me? In a Girl Scout uniform!" She teetered her head back and forth. "Not a chance; no siree, bub! Besides, I'm too old to be in the Girl Scouts."

"I think you can be a member up to eighteen." He added. "I think you would look adorable in one of those uniforms."

Kit shook her head, then walked over to the bookcase with the rag and furniture polish in hand. As she began to rub vigorously, she muttered under her breath. "Not me; not a chance. I wouldn't be caught dead in one of those girlie uniforms."

***

Three days later, Kit stood at the entrance gate of the house of Mr. and Mrs. Hamilton. The large picturesque house seemed a bit ominous as she stood in front of the large wrought-iron security gates. But that was the least of her concerns. Dressed in a sea-green skirt, a bow tie, a sash filled with merit badges, and a matching beret with the Girl Scouts logo, Kit stood there in disbelief. As he had done many times in the past, Steele had talked her into this masquerade. She turned to Steele who was sitting in his car in the distance and shook her fist. Steele laughed and motioned for her to ring the entrance gate bell. Being around 10:00 am, Steele figured Mr. Hamilton would be at his office, so Eve would most likely be the only one home; unless they had a butler or maid.

As Kit stood with a box in her hands, supposedly filled with mint chip cookies, she pressed the button and then was alerted as a voice came over the intercom.

"Hamilton residence; may I help you?"

Kit cleared her throat. "Yes, may I come up to the house? I'm selling Girl Scout cookies."

Silence sat over the intercom when finally, someone spoke back. "I'm sorry, but Mrs. Hamilton said she does not want any cookies today."

Kit thought quickly. "But wait, I was at the Main Street offices of Mr. Hamilton the other day. He told his secretary to give me your address and that his wife would buy a box or two from me."

Silence once again sat over the intercom. "Very well," returned the voice. "When the gate opens, please walk up to the front door and I will greet you here."

She turned and looked towards Steele with a tentative smile, as the gates began to open. She walked through a rose-filled garden walkway and up to the house. Before she could knock on the door, it swung open. It was Eve Hamilton.

Eve looked down upon her with annoyance. "I can't believe my husband gave you our address and pawned this off on me. Anyway, what are you selling?"

Kit took off her beret and moved in closer. "It's me, Mrs. Hamilton," she said in a hushed tone. "It's me, Kit."

As she focused on Kit's face, her eyes grew wide. "Oh, my goodness!" Eve stepped onto the porch and quickly closed the door behind her. "What are you doing here?"

"You hadn't gotten in touch with Mr. Steele in a few days, and he needs you to get some information for him."

"Actually, I was going to call or come by your office tomorrow. However, it was a little risky for you to come to our home like this."

Kit opened her arms in presenting fashion. "Seriously? Look at me. Nobody who knows who I am would ever recognize me in this outfit."

Eve glanced at her from head to toe. "No, I guess you are right. That outfit doesn't fit your usual tomboy attire. Tell me quickly what Mr. Steele needs; I don't want my maid to get suspicious."

"The bottom line is Rick needs you to look into your husband's appointment book for the next two weeks. He wants to know when and where he and his secretary Miss Wilson will be out of the office together. Like at a business or luncheon meeting. He wants to be able to observe them together outside of the office. Also, can you write down Miss Wilson's address? He also plans on staking out her house to see if the two of them are having rendezvous at her place."

Eve nodded her head. "Very good, I see he is on the case. I'll get that information for you, and I will be by the office tomorrow around this same time. And for the sake of appearance, I'll just tell my maid I wasn't interested in the type of cookies you had to offer." Eve scanned her attire once more. "If it was me, I wouldn't be caught dead in an outfit like that."

As Kit began to walk away, she muttered under her breath. "I said the very same thing."

Kit walked over to the car and got in. Steele had a comical smile on his face. "So, did you sell any cookies?"

She snarled her nose. "Very funny, Mr. Jack Benny. Next time, you get to wear the stupid outfit."

Steele started the car and began to drive off. "I assume you spoke with Mrs. Hamilton."

"Yeah, I did. But it took some quick thinking otherwise I would have never made it inside those gates. The maid answered and was trying to get rid of me. When I got to the door, Eve Hamilton answered. At first, she did not recognize me, but I took off my beret and told her who I was. I told her what you wanted, and she said she would bring it to you tomorrow around 10:00 am. It's funny, but she looked so different without all that makeup. But in my opinion, she looked much better without all that gunk on her face—more natural."

"That's my preference in women also." A look of remembrance drew upon his face. "Rachel was so beautiful; she didn't need any of that makeup. She would just put on a little lipstick."

"Yes, she was very pretty by the photos you showed me."

"As soon as we get that information from Eve, I'll start to spy on them to see if I can see any romantic gestures between them. Which reminds me, after you have lunch, can you pick up three rolls of film for me? We have three suspects so we need plenty. And remember, I use the Kodak 35 RF. I want the black and white film, not the new color film. The color film doesn't have good clarity."

"Yes, I'll remember." She playfully rustled her skirt. "Should I go to the drug store to buy the film in my fancy new outfit?"

"Only if you want to draw attention to yourself."

"I was only joshing. Besides I wouldn't want anyone who knows me to see me in this outfit."

Steele turned with a smile. "You mean someone like, Jake?"

Kit held a pursed smile. "You're never going to stop teasing me about him, are you?"

He half-laughed. "No, it's too much fun to see your face turn beet red."

"It does not turn beet red!" she snapped. "Jake is my friend— that's all we are."

"Okay, you're friends—for now."

As they continued back to the office, Kit sat with the slightest grin and with the words 'for now' residing in her mind.

Chapter Five

The next morning Eve Hamilton arrived promptly at 10:00 am. As she opened the door to the office, she almost ran into Kit who was leaving on an errand.

Eve Hamilton scanned her up and down. "What, no Girl Scout outfit today?" she said with sarcasm trailing in her voice.

Kit shook her head in the negative. "No, thank goodness my Girl Scout days are over." She wiggled her pant pockets. "Back to my regular *'tomboy'* duds."

Eve stepped into the office and turned to Steele looking out the window.

"Taking in the sights this morning, Mr. Steele?"

He pointed down to the street. "Have you noticed that Stan the flower man just seems so content with his life? He just sells flowers all day, but he always has a smile on his face and greets everyone who walks by his cart. He's been working that corner like clockwork for the past fifteen years."

Eve Hamilton held a look of indifference. "Well, I suppose somebody has to do those kinds of jobs. Why do you even care about some street vendor anyway? You really are a Boy Scout caring about people the way you do."

Steele moved from the window and sat at his desk. "Caring about people is being a Boy Scout? I think caring about people is just showing your humanity."

Eve shrugged her shoulders. "If you say so. But I have found that the more you care, the more chances people will hurt you."

Steele stared at Eve in studying fashion. There was something hidden in that statement that made him feel she was badly hurt in her past.

Steele opened the subject case file. "Were you able to get that information from your husband's appointment book?"

She reached into her handbag. "Yes, I was. While he was in the shower, I went into his office and his appointment book was laying on his desk. He has a business lunch appointment on Friday at noon at the Yorkshire café. Anytime it's a business meeting, Miss Wilson will be with him."

Steele wrote a note in the file. "Anything else?"

"Yes, I saw he is scheduled for a round of golf next Tuesday at the Lakeside Golf & Country Club. He also uses this time to meet with clients in a more relaxed atmosphere. And remember, that is where Darlene Thomas works so you might see her there also."

Steele glanced to the side, then returned his focus. "That might work out very well; I can kill two birds with one stone. If I can see them together in a casual setting, I'll make note of how they interact with each other."

"Oh yes, that reminds me; I need to place your name on the guest list at the club. With a member's recommendation, like mine, guests can gain entrance to look at the grounds and all the facilities. They will take you on a tour of the golf courses, the main clubhouse, outdoor restaurant, and so forth. Once you complete the tour, you are free to view all the facilities by yourself. Just give the entrance gate concierge your name and say you are a guest of Eve Hamilton and he will let you in. Also, make sure you dress appropriately."

"Sounds like a plan. However, I just remembered something; I may need Kit to go with me. There may be times when I am speaking to someone and I will need Kit to stay within an earshot of the conversations your husband or Miss Thomas is having. Can she be placed on the guestlist also?"

Eve took out a pen and wrote a note to herself. "Yes, I will make sure your visit includes a guest." Eve closed her purse. "Have you done any other investigating so far?"

"Yes, I went to your husband's office on Main Street. I made an appointment as a potential client looking to set up a trust fund on behalf of my sister. I was there to observe both your husband and Miss Wilson."

Eve sat back in the chair and crossed her legs. "And what did you find out?"

"Well for one, I can see why you might think your husband would be interested in Miss Wilson—she is very attractive. At first, I asked her some general questions, but was moving the conversation in the direction I wanted. After she made a comment which opened the door, I then asked her about Mr. Hamilton's marriage, and she became a bit guarded. That could mean two things. One, it could simply mean she feels it's her job as his secretary to not divulge information. Or secondly, she is having an affair with him and my questioning of your marriage struck a chord with her—I'm not sure."

"And my husband?" she said with a raised brow.

"Well, Mr. Hamilton is an interesting man. He seems very sure of himself and his knowledge as a lawyer. I did make a few comments about Miss Wilson being attractive, and that's when he became defensive. But to me, it wasn't the type of possessiveness you see when someone is in a dating relationship. To me, it was more like a brother being protective of a younger sister. Again, that was my observation in the short amount of time I was there."

"Was there anything else you noticed?"

"There was. When I was in the office with your husband, he showed me a vintage rifle he has in a gun case."

Eve waved her hand in shooing fashion. "Yes, him and his guns; he is so obsessed with them. Sometimes I think he cares more for those guns than me."

"I then asked your husband if he had more guns, and he said he had more at his house in Southport. However, after he made that statement, he glanced to the side in thought. I felt there was more to his answer than he was letting on."

"You and me both. He has a much bigger display case full of them at the Southport house where they are locked up like Fort Knox. Like you, I have also felt he may have more guns or other valuables hidden in the house. I say this because one time we were spending the weekend there, and he had a few of his former college buddies visiting. In passing by his study, I heard them talking about the guns. I heard my husband whisper something to the men, and then he walked to the door and locked it. I tried to listen to what they were saying with my ear to the door. I did hear one man say, 'that's an amazing secret', but that was all I could make out. That's why I feel he may have more guns or valuable items hidden somewhere." A somber look etched across her face. "I guess you could say I was a little hurt by it. Here I am his wife, yet these old college friends of his know this 'secret' and not me."

Steele took a mental note of Eve's statement. "Thank you for the information about your husband's appointments. I will follow up on these and let you know my progress on the investigation."

"Thank you; I'll keep an eye on my husband's schedule and let you know when he will be going to the house in Southport. I will need to make reservations at the hotel, plus there are several things I need to do in preparation for that trip."

"Very good, just get in contact with me when you have that information. Which reminds me; what if I need to get in touch with you? I don't think it would make sense for Kit to show up at your house in that Girl Scouts uniform again."

"Actually, I have been thinking about that. How about you call the house and let the phone ring once, then you hang up. I will know it is you, and about ten minutes later, I'll call you back."

"Very clever, I like it."

Eve Hamilton walked out of Steele's office with a strange look of contentment laying on her face. Steele didn't know quite what to make of it, or if he should be worried about it.

*****

Kit returned from running her errands and set a few items in the supply closet.

"I got those rolls of film you wanted. And yes, I got the black and white film."

"Thanks, Kit; you can keep the change."

She smiled. "That's good because I've been meaning to get me one of those root-beer floats they have at the soda fountain in the drug store." She looked towards the open file on his desk. "Was there anything new with the Hamilton case?"

"As a matter of fact, there is. We will be going out to the Lakeside Golf & Country Club next Tuesday."

She directed a questioning stare. "We?"

"Yes, because I am now recognized by Mr. Hamilton as Mr. Reid, I need to make sure he doesn't think I'm there other than to consider a membership. Therefore, I will probably try to keep my distance when he is around. I need you to listen in on any conversation he has with Miss Thomas. If they are having an affair, there are always tell-tell signs of affection towards one another. Plus, while he is there, they might make plans for a secret rendezvous." Steele paused for a moment with a growing smile on his face.

Kit took notice. "Okay, I know that look. And it usually doesn't bode well for me."

He chuckled. "You know me too well. I was thinking, we're going to have to get you a tea dress."

Her eyes grew wide. "A tea dress?" She shook her head. "No sir, not me!"

"Look, if we are considering a membership at that high-class country club, then we have to dress the part as if we have money."

Kit shook her head in disgust. "Great, from a Girl Scouts uniform to a prissy debutant dress. What's next, a monkey suit?"

Steele directed a raised brow. "Hey, you never know. I hear they have these fancy fashion shows in France where women wear tuxedos."

"Well, we don't live in France so a tea dress is as far as I will go."

He glanced down at her weathered tennis shoes. "We're also going to have to get you a nice pair of penny loafers to go along with that dress."

"Awe come on! I'll never use that outfit but this one time."

"What about church? You could go to church in a nice pretty dress."

"God doesn't look at the outside of people, He looks at their heart."

"Then what about Jake? One day he might ask you on a date and you might need a nice dress for the occasion."

A brush of a smile lifted her lips. "Well, if he *were to ask me*, I don't plan on going to any place needing any dress—I'll just go as I am. "

"Well, this isn't costing you a penny, so buck it up kiddo; I need you on this one."

Kit begrudgingly nodded her head. "Alright, but do I get a bonus for doing this?"

"Your bonus is that you get a brand-new dress and a new pair of shoes—that's your bonus."

She nodded her head. "Yes, I guess you're right."

"Speaking of your job; I need you to make up a file on Darlene Thomas. She's the next focus in this investigation."

Chapter Six

A week later Steele drove over to where Kit lives with her foster family. He didn't want her to have to ride her bike to the office in her dress. As she walked out the door and got into the car, he was taken back by how different she looked. Like a proud father, the edges of his mouth lifted a smile.

"My goodness young lady; you look so grown up in that dress."

"Okay, tell me the truth; I look stupid, don't I?"

"Stupid is not the word for how you look." He glanced at her once more, then started the engine. "You look very pretty and much more mature."

She ran her hand down the back of her hair. "Believe it or not my foster mother saw I was getting all dressed up and she wanted to curl my hair. It was kind of weird as she never pays any attention to me in that way. When she was styling my hair, it was almost like I could feel some emotion coming from her towards me. Then she hugged me and told me to have a good time at my outing." Kit lowered her gaze. "I don't know, maybe it was good for us. Maybe our relationship will be better from now on."

Steele nodded. "Sometimes that's all it takes. Maybe she was waiting for a moment where she had some common ground with you. Maybe you could ask her to do more girlie stuff with you."

"Okay, let's not get carried away. I'm still me; you know."

She scanned Steele's attire. "Speaking of being dressed to the nines; you're looking awfully sharp in your dress trousers and a polo shirt. I've never seen you wear that outfit."

"I bring it out for special occasions such as this."

"Speaking of occasions, did anything happen when you spied on Mr. Hamilton and Miss Wilson at their luncheon meeting last Friday?"

"No, not a single thing. Mr. Hamilton seemed more concerned with the person who I assumed was a potential client. And Miss Wilson mainly took notes. After finishing their lunch, they drove back to the office and that was it."

"So anyway, back to our mission for today at the country club. Who am I?"

He turned with a questioning stare. "What do you mean, who are you?"

"You said I am to play your niece, but what's my name? It's not like I can use my real name."

"That's right, I forgot all about that. Thank you for reminding me otherwise I would have called you Kit."

"Yep, Kit's the name, adventures my game!"

"Not today—not in *that* dress. You can be adventurous, but in an investigative way, and in a lady-like manner. Think classy, high society, debutant..., think Eve Hamilton."

"Yeah, I don't think I can pull that off. Just the way that woman walks, it's as if she is walking on air."

Steele nodded his head. "Yes, she does walk that way. Anyway, do you have a name you would like to be called?"

She glanced out the corner of her eye. "How about Kimberly? Kimberly Lawson sounds like a girl who would have a membership to a country club. Also, it begins with the letter, 'K', so I will naturally respond to a similar sounding name."

He nodded in approval. "Alright, Kimberly it is. Also, make sure you have a list of activities you enjoy doing because they will probably ask you. You can't say you enjoy tadpole fishing down by the creek in your bare feet. Or soapbox derby racing with the boys down Coulter's grade. Girls your age with money go shopping, they go English-style horseback riding, and enjoy croquet."

"Really? All that stuff sounds so drab and boring. Oh, and by the way, I used to win most of those soapbox derby races," she said with a winning smile.

Steele continued to drive, then turned into the driveway to the Lakeside Golf & Country Club. He drove up to the entrance and was greeted by a well-dressed man at the guard booth.

"May I assist you?" the man greeted, with an English inflection in his voice.

Steele drummed up his best uppity accent. "Yes, good man. My niece and I have been cordially invited by Mrs. Eve Hamilton to view the facility as we consider membership."

The guard took hold of a clipboard. "And your name, sir?"

"Yes, Jeffrey Reid, and my niece Kimberly Lawson."

He scanned the list of names. "Yes, there it is. It says, Jeffrey Reid and guest."

The man pulled a lever as the gate began to open. "When you get to the parking area, there will be a building which says, Lakeside Club House. That is where you will sign in and be greeted by Miss Thomas or one of our concierges."

Steele politely tilted his head. "Very well, you have a chipper good day."

The man tilted his head in return. "Thank you, sir, you as well."

As they began to drive towards the parking area, Kit turned with an inquisitive stare. "A chipper good day? Who are you? I couldn't even recognize you by the way you were talking."

"In this business, you have to wear many hats. This is my high society hat."

Kit shook her head. "I guess so. But I don't have to talk like that, do I?"

"No, but try to use big words. That always impresses these types of people."

Steele parked the car and the two of them got out and headed to the clubhouse entrance.

He glanced around the facility. "Be on the lookout for Mr. Hamilton. Eve said he will be here for a round of golf and some socializing."

They entered the door and were greeted by a woman at the desk. "Welcome to Lakeside Golf & Country Club. I am Darlene Thomas. And your names?"

Steele pulled Kit to his side as she was shadowed behind him. "My name is Jeffrey Reid, and this is my lovely niece, Kimberly. We are here to peruse the facilities for possible membership."

Darlene Thomas took hold of a couple of brochures and handed one to each of them.

"The brochure goes into depth about our facilities, but I will be your guide for a hands-on tour."

Steele glanced around when he thought he saw Mr. Hamilton talking with some men near the Pro shop. He thought to avoid that area.

"Can we start with a tour of the golf courses? I hear you have some world-class players who are members here."

"Yes, most definitely," she said proudly. "Our pro is a former PGA Tour member with many awards to his name."

Miss Thomas walked through the clubhouse as she explained all aspects of the amenities offered to club members. They went outside and began walking towards a viewing point that over-looked the courses. As they continued walking, a gentle breeze kept catching the hem of Kit's flared and pleated dress. With the hem resting at her knees, the strange feeling of the dress had her hands swatting at it with reckless abandon. Steele took notice of her antics, so he pointed to her dress and directed to her a stern telling look.

"Is a bee bothering you, Kimberly? I figure it must be a bee considering that would be *the only reason* you would be swatting at the hem of your dress."

Kit caught his stern hint. "Yes, you're right, it was a bee. I was able to get the bee away from me, so I have no reason to swat at it anymore."

They continued on their tour of the grounds, as Miss Thomas pointed to the Pro shop and the Olympic size swimming pool. Kit gazed at the shimmering pool and watched a few members bask in its cool waters. *What I wouldn't give to get out of this stupid dress and take a dip in the cool waters of that pool.*

The tour proceeded indoors and over to a full gym with work-out equipment for the men, and slenderizing equipment for the ladies. Miss Thomas pointed out both the men's and women's locker room, then drifted back into the clubhouse and over to the outdoor restaurant with covered seating.

"Well, that pretty much sums it up," she said. "I left you here at the outdoor restaurant in case you are thirsty or want something to eat. With your guest's name tag, you are entitled to a complimentary drink. And as I mentioned before, you are free to walk the grounds at your leisure. Everything is available to you, except the golf course which you must have a prior reservation." She turned to Kit. "Kimberly, did you bring a swimsuit? The pool is also available to you as a guest."

Kit shook her head. "No, but thank you. It looks very inviting, but maybe another time if we choose to get membership into the club."

Steele pointed to a table of empty seats. "Miss Thomas, if you don't have to be anywhere in the next few minutes, I'd like to talk to you some more."

She looked at her wristwatch. "I do have another tour coming up, but I guess I can talk for a few minutes."

One of the waitresses came to the table as Steele and Kit ordered a drink.

Steele scanned around the facility. "The country club is very impressive. You have just about everything a person could want. How long have you worked here?"

"I've worked here for over four years. I started as a waitress and moved up to customer service manager."

He glanced around once more. "I see you have a number of high society members here. For example, I believe I saw Mr. Randall Hamilton near the Pro shop."

"Yes, I assumed you probably knew him considering that his wife, Eve, was the one who made you a guest to view the facilities. Do you know Randall personally?"

"Actually, we met last week at his office. I may be hiring him to set up a trust fund for my sister and her children. He appears to be a nice gentleman. How about you? Do you know Mr. Hamilton very well?"

"I do know him, and on occasion we have friendly conversations. As far as being nice and a gentleman, my dealings with him have been cordial." She glanced to the side. "However, I only know this one side of him. Others might have a different opinion in their dealings with him."

Steele knew this was his opening. "Tell me, Miss Thomas; why did you make that statement about other people's opinion in dealings with Mr. Hamilton? Is there something I need to know? I mean, if I am going to be hiring his law firm, I want to make sure I'm dealing with a man of integrity."

"I really shouldn't have said anything. I guess you could say it was a knee-jerk reaction to a past event."

"Go on," he prompted.

She looked around. "Okay, but please keep this in confidence. Yes, in some ways he is a very nice man. And as far as you hiring him, his law firm is legitimate. However, he lives his life as one would dress to a masquerade ball—he has two faces. You see, my brother Daniel is in the construction business and has worked on many building projects in the downtown area. He had an opportunity to invest and branch out into the building and acquisitions aspect. There was an older block of buildings on the east side, which my brother and a friend were going to be partners in acquiring the property. He was going to renovate the buildings himself and then lease them out. It was going to be very lucrative for him. At a point in the acquisitions process, suddenly Mr. Hamilton's law firm became involved. They claimed some existing building codes were prohibiting my brother and his partner from acquiring the property in its current state. Apparently, at one time some of the buildings were classified as part residential/part commercial. So in order to purchase them, my brother would have to go through a lengthy process of getting the codes changed through City Hall. The process was filled with red-tape, and with Mr. Hamilton's law firm filing injunctions and causing roadblocks, it was costing my brother too much time and money, so he had to give up the fight. In the end, Mr. Hamilton's firm won and my brother could not acquire the property."

Miss Thomas dabbed a brimming tear from the corner of her eye. She cleared her throat and then continued. "Even worse than not getting the property, the bad press in the local newspapers of fighting against Mr. Hamilton's well-respected law firm, caused my brother's construction company to lose bids, and soon his company went bankrupt. He currently has a job as a foreman for a different company, but basically, he lost everything. The irony of this story is that a short time after the lawsuit, suddenly Mr. Hamilton's law firm finds a loophole in the building codes. That same property was then sold to another construction company that is renovating those buildings the same way my brother wanted to. I found this information out from a friend of mine who works close to Mr. Hamilton. Well, as it turned out, the company that now won the bid, is backed by an investment company. And guess what... Randall Hamilton is a stockholder in that investment company where he is making big money from those stock holdings. That's why I say that Mr. Hamilton is two-faced. He seems so nice on the outside, but on the inside, he can be very cunning."

Steele studied her for a moment. "You seem to be very bitter about it."

"Yes, for my brother's sake, I am. I have to deal with people like Mr. Hamilton because of my job here at the club, so I treat him cordially like anyone else. It's a little hard because he seems to go out of his way to have friendly conversations with me. I think he feels bad about what happened, so this is his way of somehow making reconciliation. But I'm not the one he needs to make reconciliation with. He needs to talk things out with my brother, Daniel." Miss Thomas rose to her feet. "I need to get back to work, but enjoy the rest of your day, Mr. Reid. The brochure explains the cost and how to enroll in membership."

Steele smiled. "Thank you for your time, Miss Thomas. And don't worry, anything that you have said in confidence, I will keep in confidence."

She pressed out a smile. "Thank you; I appreciate it."

As Miss Thomas walked away, Steele and Kit ordered a club sandwich to share and a couple of sodas.

As he was just about finished, he turned to her. "And what do you think, *Miss Kimberly*? Do you think you would enjoy a place like this?"

Kit caught his playful assertion. "Well, *Uncle Jeffrey,* a girl could get used to something like this. However," she said looking around. "It's a bit too stuffy for my taste. When we were on the tour and we walked by a couple of girls my age, they forced a 'polite' smile which quickly faded once we passed them. At my school, we call those people two-faced backstabbers."

He nodded his head and looked around. "Yes, I do know what you mean."

Kit casually slurped the remaining soda at the bottom of the bottle.

Steele leaned forward and whispered in a hushed tone. "You may not want to slurp your soda. I don't think this is the kind of place where people slurp."

She nodded her head. "Yep, and that's why I would never join a club like this. Slurping is part of the fun of having a soda pop." Kit then slurped loudly for the effect.

Steele smiled and just shook his head. Suddenly, his eyes caught Mr. Hamilton walking their way while talking with another gentleman. As he approached, he stopped and turned towards Steele with a look of recollection.

"Mr. Reid, am I correct?"

Steele extended his hand. "Yes, Mr. Hamilton, that's correct."

"When you were in my office the other day, I said that perhaps we would run into each other someday. I just didn't think it would be so soon." His eyes drifted over to Kit. "And who is this charming young lady?"

"That's my niece, Kimberly." Steele pointed his finger in presenting fashion. "Kimberly, this is Mr. Hamilton from the law firm I went to."

Mr. Hamilton extended his hand when a look of panic rose upon Kit's face. She realized her roughworked hands would give away that she was a working girl.

She waved him off. "So sorry, but I have been fighting a terrible cold and I wouldn't want you to catch it. But it is nice meeting you, Mr. Hamilton."

He smiled. "You too, Miss Kimberly. And take care of that cold."

She politely smiled. "Thank you, I will."

He turned to Steele. "I presume by the guest badge on your shirt that you are considering a membership with the club?"

"Yes, and what a fine club it is. If I do decide to join, then I will need to brush up on my game. Too many hook shots on the putting green."

Mr. Hamilton half-laughed. "Yes, I definitely know what you mean. Good to see you again, Mr. Reid." He tipped his sun visor towards Kit. "Miss Kimberly."

As he walked off, Steele turned to Kit. "I think I will follow Mr. Hamilton at a distance. Even though it doesn't appear Miss Thomas is the one he is having the affair with given her bitterness, we still need to keep an eye on her. In the meantime, I will see where Mr. Hamilton is going. Maybe there is another woman here at the club he is involved with."

"No problem, I'll be here."

Steele pulled a quarter from his pant pocket. "Here, in case you want another soda to slurp."

She smiled. "Thanks, and don't worry; no more slurping."

As Kit motioned for the waitress to take her order, a woman came into her view. The woman, dressed in a business suit, then motioned to someone in the restaurant. As Kit turned to see who the other woman was, she realized it was Miss Thomas. A table next to where Kit was sitting opened up. The two women greeted with a friendly hug and sat down at the table.

In the meantime, Steele had followed Mr. Hamilton who headed towards the parking lot. He had the valet get his car and he drove away. Steele began to make his way back to get Kit when a shocking sight stopped him in his tracks. He quickly ducked out of view and sat on a bench just outside the entrance of the restaurant. As he peered around the entrance barrier, what he was seeing caused his mind to swirl a mile a minute.

So that's who Miss Thomas was talking about. And that makes sense as she said a friend of hers works with Mr. Hamilton. But why are they meeting here at the club?

Back inside, Kit listened in on their conversation as the two women engaged in some pleasantries and general conversation. Then they both looked around as if to make sure no one was within hearing range.

"I'm glad you could meet me," the woman told Miss Thomas. "I had to wait until Mr. Hamilton left the country club."

"Yes May, I'm glad you could make it. Mr. Hamilton isn't going back to the office right now, is he?"

"He has another appointment so he shouldn't be going back anytime soon. But even if he does, I told him I needed to take an extra-long lunch for an errand I need to run."

"Good thinking. So May, did you get the information I need for the purchase?"

"Yes, I was finally able to get it. It took me some time and research, but I finally found the right model."

May casually reached across the table and handed Miss Thomas a note.

She looked it over. "Okay, good. I know someone who knows a guy who has knowledge on how to acquire items like this."

"And who is that?"

Miss Thomas hesitated momentarily. "My brother."

"You're brother, Daniel? You told him about what we're doing?"

"I needed to; I think he needs to be involved in this. For example, when I mentioned I needed to find someone to purchase a certain type of gun, he volunteered to get it. He said he would ask the guy he knows for me. My brother knows a guy who was formerly in the military. That guy has a lot of knowledge about military guns and guns in general. He said the guy had fallen on hard times and was living at someplace called The Alley. Then when I mention that the gun was intended for Mr. Hamilton, he quipped to make sure that it was plenty loaded."

May opened her purse and pulled out an envelope. "Here is my portion for the purchase. If it costs more, let me know."

Miss Thomas glanced inside the envelope. "No, this should be enough."

May closed her purse. "I'll let you know the exact date and time when Mr. Hamilton will be at his home in Southport. This has to be a complete surprise. I am in contact with the person who will let us into the side door. She doesn't know about what we are planning, and as far as she knows, we are just there to help decorate the entertainment room for the upcoming party."

Darlene looked intently into her eyes. "Are you sure you want to do this? I have my reasons which you fully know, but you work side by side with the man. You have also seen two sides of him, whereas I have only seen one—a deceitful one."

May glanced to the side in recollection, then returned her focus. "There are two sides to everybody. I have seen that bad side of someone who was very close to me and they deeply hurt me. And because of that, now I owe a lot of money which will take me years to dig out of. Sometimes doing the unexpected can bring about reconciliation and put an end to things once and for all."

Miss Thomas gathered a look of remembrance. "I can understand where you're coming from. And you are right, there are two sides to everybody. But as you know, Mr. Hamilton did my brother wrong and I'm still very bitter about that. But as you say, maybe this will put an end to things once and for all. And what he has coming, part of me knows he deserves it. In fact, let me be the one to do it."

A look of surprise rose on May's face. "Are you sure? I'm the one who has handled a gun at a shooting range. Even just holding one can make a person shaky."

"No, I think I need to be the one to do it. I think I need to put an end to this, and have it coming from my hand."

May rose to her feet. "If there isn't anything else, I'll talk to you soon. Let me know when you have acquired it, and in the meantime, I will find out from his appointment book when he plans to be in Southport for the weekend. We need to do this very soon, as this may be our only chance. From what I have heard, it appears that his wife is looking to divorce him soon. When this all comes down with the divorce, we won't have the opportunity to do it. I told you when Mr. Hamilton had me place the Will back into his safe, I got a look at it. I saw the new revisions that are now a part of the Will. With the new changes, it will be interesting to see Mrs. Hamilton's reaction to see what she gets. The woman is so greedy. She doesn't deserve a dime if you ask me."

"I agree. As soon as Daniel talks to the guy and purchases it, I'll let you know."

As May Wilson headed for the exit, Steele tucked out of view. When he saw that Miss Thomas had gone back inside the club-house, he made his way over to where Kit was sitting.

As Steele looked at Kit, her eyes grew large with an unusual look upon her face.

"What's wrong? You have a strange look on your face."

She looked around so no one was within hearing distance. "You are not going to believe what I just heard. Remember how you said you thought this case was going to have a lot of twists and turns? Well, the case just took a doozy of a turn!"

He leaned in closer. "Why, what do you mean?"

"I think those two women are planning on killing Mr. Hamilton!"

A look of pessimism drew upon his face. "What? No, that can't be. Tell me everything that was said, and slowly."

"Okay, first they began with general chit-chat. But then Miss Thomas asked this woman whose name is May..."

Steele interjected. "Yes, I know who she is. That was May Wilson, Mr. Hamilton's secretary and the one I spoke to the other day. Anyway, go on with what you were saying."

"Then Miss Thomas asked if Miss Wilson had the information. Miss Wilson then gave her a note with something written on it. I couldn't see what it was because I had my back to them. Then they mentioned something about purchasing a gun. Miss Wilson said it needed to be a surprise. Miss Thomas then said something like, she would like to be the one to do it. Miss Wilson responded and said, 'I am the one who has handled guns at the shooting range. Even just handling a gun can make a person shaky.' My eyes must have bugged out of my head when I heard her say that. Miss Thomas then said that resolution has been a long time coming. I think she was referring to her bitterness against Mr. Hamilton. Miss Wilson then gave Miss Thomas an envelope of money. Miss Thomas told her that it would be her brother who would be the one to get the gun. Then Miss Thomas said it was necessary to get him involved, as he knows a guy who can tell him where to get the gun. That guy had a ton of knowledge about guns, and he believes he was living at The Alley. Miss Thomas then said her brother commented, to make sure it was fully loaded. After that, Miss Wilson said they needed to do it soon. She said Mrs. Hamilton may be planning to divorce him soon and so they need to do it before the divorce proceedings happen and they won't have the opportunity."

Steele sat with a blank stare laying upon his face. "I can't believe this. There has to be another explanation."

Kit sipped the last of her soda. "I'm just telling you what I heard."

"No, I'm not questioning what you heard. I just don't believe that the two of them would be planning something like that—especially Miss Wilson. I have a very good sense when it comes to determining someone's character. I just can't imagine her being involved in something like that. She was so personable, attractive, and nice."

An inquisitive look drew upon Kit's face. "Are you sweet on this woman? You only mentioned Miss Wilson not being involved in this. There are two women in this situation, yet you only seem concerned about Miss Wilson."

"Okay, don't go reading into things. All I'm saying is when I spoke to May, she didn't seem like the type of person to be involved in a conspiracy to kill someone. Besides, if there is someone capable of doing it, it would be Miss Thomas. She has a motive because of what Mr. Hamilton did to her brother. You could tell she was very bitter about it when we talked to her. Bitter enough to want to kill him? —I don't know. And as far as May is concerned, maybe Mr. Hamilton has done her wrong as well. Or maybe this has something to do with Mr. Hamilton's Will."

Kit tapped her forehead with the palm of her hand. "Oh man, speaking of the Will, I forgot about that part. In the conversation, Miss Wilson said that when Mr. Hamilton was placing the Will back in the safe, that she got a look at it. She then mentioned someone about the new revisions and that Mrs. Hamilton is going to be surprised to find out about the changes. May then said that Eve Hamilton was greedy and she didn't deserve it."

Steele sat in deep thought. "A theory just entered my mind. Perhaps May had the Will altered to make her one of the beneficiaries. And that's why she said they needed to do it before Mrs. Hamilton files for divorce. Because the minute Eve files for divorce, Mr. Hamilton will get that Will out of the safe because it will be used in the divorce proceedings. However, if Mr. Hamilton were dead, no one would know that the Will was altered without his consent. The benefactor page of the Will doesn't have signatures, only the last page has to be signed by the testator, or Mr. Hamilton in this case. Also, it doesn't have to be notarized, it only needs a signature of a witness to the Will." Steele suddenly drew a thought. "Wait, maybe it was May who Mr. Hamilton had as his witness to the Will. When I spoke to him, he talked about her in high regard and he trusted her very much. And as far as Darlene Thomas is concerned, she and May might have agreed upon a portion of the money, along with her brother Daniel. And at some point, May was able to get into the safe and altered the Will. This all sounds so crazy, but on the other hand, there is a driving force in this world that makes people do things you never thought they would. That driving force is called money."

"So, what do we do?"

"We need to get positive proof. All we have is a conversation between the two women. I need to find out when they are planning this and catch them with the gun. And speaking of guns; we need to find out a little more about Miss Thomas' brother Daniel.

For example, what does he look like and what kind of car does he drive?"

"Why do we need to know that about the brother?"

"I need that information to positively identify him. When I go to The Alley and talk to John, I'll ask him if he knows a guy who has a lot of knowledge about guns. Since May and Darlene wouldn't want the gun to be traced back to them, it makes sense they wouldn't want to buy the gun at a regular gun shop. That man at The Alley probably knows someone who sells guns under the table. Then once we find out when they plan on doing this, I will alert the Southport police to be on hand for the possible arrest. Before that, I will go into the Southport Police Station and talk with them. Hopefully, they don't have any close ties to members of my old department otherwise their opinion of me might be tainted. I also need to have another talk with Eve Hamilton. I need her to find out for me the next time her husband will be at the house in Southport working alone, or at the very least with Poppy Sorenson."

Kit's eyes grew wide. "Oh, sorry, I forgot about something else. One thing that Miss Wilson said, is she knows someone who can allow them access into the Southport house. Also, they will be there for his party to help set up decorations. Do you think it could be this Poppy person?"

"Maybe, and that would make sense because this Poppy does have access to the house. Eve Hamilton said she is there all the time, as she sets things up for his meetings or other events. This is starting to sound so crazy that all of them would be involved in something like this. Maybe it's like that movie that came out a few years ago called, Murder on the Orient Express. After investigating, it turned out that everyone on the train was involved in the man's murder. The thing is, I've been in this business long enough to know that when it comes to greed, people will do just about anything. Kit, you know the Bible pretty well. Doesn't it say something about greed?"

"It says a lot about greed. But the verse I know the best is, 'The love of money is the root of all evil.' And if these women are planning something like this, then all of them are very evil."

Steele rose from his chair. "I will talk with Eve Hamilton and ask her to check her husband's schedule. However, I'm not going to tell her what we know about this conspiracy to kill him. If these women are truly planning something like this, I need to be at the Southport house on that day and catch them with the gun. If I tell Mrs. Hamilton what we know, she may get scared and alert her husband as to what these women are planning."

"Yes, I agree."

"However, we'll have to put this investigation on hold for a week. I have that hearing I was subpoenaed to go to on one of my old cases when I was on the force."

"Oh yeah, I remember you saying that."

"But when I get back, we'll make our plans for the next part of this investigation.

I said this case was going to have a lot of twists and turns, but I never expected anything like a possible conspiracy to kill someone."

As they got on their way, Steele felt a twinge of anxiety twist in his gut. Like a ship heading into treacherous icy waters, he wondered when it might hit that proverbial iceberg.

Chapter Seven

A week later, Steele told Kit he would be back as he was going to breakfast at the café. When he arrived, he opened the door and walked directly to the newsstand, and got a paper. As he sat down, Betsy walked over to greet him.

"Morning, Mr. Steele."

"What did I tell you Betsy; you can call me Richard or Rick."

"I know, but my boss is very particular that we address our patrons as Mr., Mrs., or Miss.—I'm just used to it. Do you want the Monday special?"

"No, actually I'm going to change it up. I'm working on this case which all of a sudden, has taken an unexpected turn. This made me realize that in life, nothing is for sure. In turn, I think I will change from my routine and order something different. Let me have your country-fried steak with eggs over easy. But I will stick with my cup of coffee, of course."

Betsy smiled. "Yes, I have the carafe ready with a fresh pot. And I'll get your breakfast right up for you."

"Thank you. Oh, and as always, a dozen of your assorted donuts."

She smiled. "Yes, I'll get those packed up for you."

Steele proceeded to eat his breakfast while reading some of the local news. After he was finished, he decided to chat with Stan the flower man, who was setting up his flower cart for the day.

Steele walked across the street and greeted him with a friendly handshake. "Morning Stan, how are you today?"

"Just dandy." He filled his lungs with the crisp morning air. "I work out in the open, and to me, every day is a new day—that's how I look at it."

"I see you sell most of the flower arrangements you bring to the stand. Getting rich?" he jested.

"You know, I make a good living doing what I love to do. How many people can make that claim? And as far as money; there's a saying I once heard that is so true. If you are not a person of character without having money, then you'll never be a person of character with it."

Steele pondered that statement. "Yes, that is quite profound. Words to live by."

"Indeed, Mr. Steele, indeed."

Steele got on his way and drove out to The Alley. As he approached with the box of donuts in his hands, John was straightening up his sleep area when Steele greeted him. "Morning John, how are you today?"

"Morning Richard. Well, that cold front we had last week put a chill to my bones, but otherwise, I'm doing fine. On the upside, I got me a part-time job in the afternoons doing some warehouse maintenance at the Firestone factory. The foreman there said if I show promise and work steady, he may have a full-time position in the near future." John looked at Steele steady in his eyes. "I'm not going to mess up this time and fall back into my ways. You have been an example to me of someone who can fall to the depths and rise above it."

"Thank you; that means a lot to me. And I know you'll make it this time; I can see it in your eyes." Steele then offered the open box of donuts, then glanced around. "By the way, you wouldn't happen to know a veteran around here who is an expert in guns?"

"You're probably talking about Greenie. He comes and goes so that's probably why you haven't ran into him."

"Greenie? Is that his real name?"

"He's called Greenie because he always wears his green fatigues from his time in the service." John pointed down the alley. "He's the fifth one down on the left."

Steele proceeded down the alleyway and gave a donut to all who wanted one. He came upon a man in green fatigues rolling up his bed military style.

"Good morning," Steele greeted and extended his hand.

The man took hold of Steele's hand with a firm shake. "Good morning, sir."

"Are you the one they call, Greenie?"

"Yes, sir. Even in these hard times, I try to wear the uniform proud."

"I'm Richard Steele. I'm a former resident here."

The man looked him over. "You don't look like it now. Glad to see some people make it out of here and make something of themselves."

"Thank you. I was here around two years ago before a friend of mine woke me up and helped me on my feet." He opened the box, "Donut?"

Greenie wiped his hand on his pants. "Thank you, don't mind if I do."

"Greenie, I hope you don't mind me asking you a few questions."

"No, sounds like a good tradeoff to me. A donut for a couple of questions."

"Did a man approach you recently about where to buy a gun? Perhaps a shop that deals in 'backroom' deals. And if he did, can you tell me what he looked like, or perhaps the kind of car he drove?"

Greenie glanced to the side then returned eye contact. "Yeah, as a matter of fact, I had two people approach me. There was a man just the other day who was asking if I knew a dealer like that. He made it sound like he was looking to buy a particular type of gun. He had brownish hair and a mustache. But as far as the car he drove, he walked into the alley so I never saw a car."

"And did you direct him to a particular shop?"

"Yes, I gave him two places. Mack's Guns on 4th, and Hanover Guns and Pawn on Central. If you're talking about backroom deals, Hanover's is probably your best bet."

Steele took out a small notepad and wrote down the information.

"Now, you mentioned someone else. What did he look like?"

"Actually, it wasn't a him, it was a her."

"A her?"

"Yeah, but she wasn't looking for a gun, she was only looking for ammo. Ammo I'm very familiar with. It was for a .38. That was the most popular handgun used in the military, and the police still use that caliber gun today."

"Tell me, given this ammo is for a very popular model gun, did you find it a strange request?"

"In some ways, yes. I mean you can get that ammo almost anywhere. But she also asked me another question that caught my attention. She asked me if all .38 guns use the same bullets. She said, for example, if the bullets would work on an older turn of the century model dating back to 1900. Anyway, I told her yes, that the ammo should work."

"Tell me, Greenie, what did this woman look like?"

He half laughed and glanced down at his fatigues. "Well, she was in camouflage, kind of like me."

Steele lowered his brow. "She was wearing army fatigues?"

"No, what I mean was she was trying to camouflage herself. She was dressed in an overcoat, her hair was covered in a bandana, and she had on those new rounded sunglasses people are wearing. She also kept looking around like she didn't want to be caught by anyone seeing her here."

"And her face and hair color?"

"As I said, her hair was covered in that bandana. But from what I could tell past her sunglasses, she appeared to be a very nice-looking woman. Again, it looked like she was making sure she was camouflaged from who she really is."

Steele nodded his head. "Thank you so much; you've been a great help."

As Steele began to walk off, Greenie shouted out, "Hey, Mr. Steele, wait a minute."

Steele returned. "Was there something else?"

"Yeah, I just remembered. She also asked if I knew a guy who could open safes. I asked her if she meant a regular locksmith or an under-the-table safecracker guy. She hesitated for a moment as if she was choosing her words carefully. She then said, to give her both types. I told her to go to Henry's Locks on Grand for a regular locksmith. And for the under-the-table guy, I told her the only one I knew is a guy named Denny. I told her she might be able to find him at Murphy's Bar on the west side of town. I advised her that Murphy's is in a rough neighborhood, so I would be careful or take someone with her. She then handed me fifty cents and left."

"Thanks, Greenie, you've been a lot of help."

As Steele finished with his donut run, he thought about the last thing Greenie had told him; how the woman asked about needing a safecracker. In turn, he thought of May Wilson.

If May wanted to alter the Will but didn't have the combination to Mr. Hamilton's safe, then she would have needed a safecracker like this man Denny who would work under the table. Greenie said she was a nice-looking woman behind the bandana and sunglasses. That would definitely fit Miss May Wilson. And as far as the bullets, maybe she and Darlene decided to split the under-the-table dealings. Daniel would get the gun for them, and May would get the bullets. Steele's eyes suddenly grew wide. *In fact, I think I remember seeing a bandana hanging on the coatrack at the office where May works.*

Steele got in his car and began to drive back to the office. That famous gut of his was at war with itself. On one hand, many things were starting to point to Miss Wilson, Miss Thomas, and possibly Daniel conspiring to kill Mr. Hamilton. And with what Greenie had told him, it only reinforced that theory. Yet the other side of his gut was telling him there was no way May Wilson could be involved in something like this. Or could it be as Kit had said, that he was beginning to be sweet on May and he didn't want to think the worst of her? As he pondered these things, only time and further investigation would confirm his gut one way or another.

Steele arrived back at the office and filled in Kit to every detail of his conversation with Greenie at The Alley.

"So, what's next?" she asked.

He pressed his lips together as he sat deep in thought. Then a look of acknowledgment rose upon his face.

"Actually, I'm going to need for you to wear your tea dress again."

Her face lit up with surprise. "We're going back to the Lakeside Country club?"

"No, only you are. I want you to keep an eye on Miss Thomas. If it was her brother Daniel who went to see Greenie about the gun, then they will probably want to talk about it. If they meet and talk at the country club, I want to know if Daniel is a part of this, or is it just May and Darlene. I know they could talk on the telephone, but maybe Daniel can't afford one. Remember he has fallen on hard times because of what Mr. Hamilton did to him. He might not want the expense of a phone bill. Now, when you are at the club, once again, listen in on her conversations. After I drop you off, then I need to make another trip to Mr. Hamilton's office. I want to see if I can get a little more information from May Wilson. And while I'm there, I can check to make sure my recollection was correct that she owns a bandana."

"But how are we going to get into the country club again? Don't those invitations from Eve Hamilton only last for that day?"

"Eve and I talked about that. Eve said she would leave what they call a standing order for a month. That way whenever we need to get in, our names will be on the list."

"When did you talk to her?"

"Last Friday evening when she called for an update. We also arranged a signal for when I need her to call me. The signal is that I will ring once and then hang up. That is her signal to call me back. That way you don't have to show up again in your Girl Scouts uniform."

Kit nodded her head. "Very clever about the signal. So, when am I going back to the country club?"

"We'll go tomorrow. In the meantime, I need to do a little research on this brother of Miss Thomas. I would like to talk to Eve Hamilton about the brother, but then she would get suspicious as to why. As far as she's concerned, we are only looking into these women as far as a possible affair with her husband. She doesn't know there is something else going on. Also, when I'm talking to May Wilson, I want to probe her about this Poppy Sorensen. She probably has dealt with her because I'm sure they have spoken whenever Mr. Hamilton needs some work-related event to be set up at the Southport house. Right now, I need to come up with a good excuse for going into the office of Mr. Hamilton again."

Kit directed a look of confidence. "I wouldn't worry about it, you'll come up with something—you always do."

*****

The next day, Steele picked up Kit once again directly from her house and they drove to the Lakeside Country Club. They were let in through the main gate and he dropped her off in front of the clubhouse.

"I'll be back in about two hours. Also, when I talked to Eve, I told her the name of Kimberly Lawson needed to be on the list, so she said she would add you." He pulled out his wallet. "Here is a dollar for you to get something to eat or drink. And don't get too used to being here. There is no way I can afford for us to become members here."

Kit rolled her eyes. "Me, wanting to be with all these prudish girls? —not a chance. However, I will say that I love that they have Fitz's root beer soda—it's the best!"

"In the meantime, try to keep an eye on Darlene. Remember, this is Mr. Hamilton's golf day, so they may talk to each other again. This whole conspiracy theory to kill him is not a sure thing. We still need to keep an eye out for the affair. I mean, that's what we were hired to do in the first place."

She nodded her head. "I got it. So, did you think of an excuse to show up at the office of Mr. Hamilton?"

A sly smile rose on his face. "I did. You know, it's the craziest thing, but I must have by accident thrown out that brochure they gave me. I guess I'm just going to have to go back over there and get another one."

Kit shook her head. "You never cease to amaze me. But I guess that's why you are such a good private eye."

"Thanks. You have a good time and keep a 'private-eye' out for Miss Thomas and Mr. Hamilton."

She smiled at his play on words. "And you have a good time too, talking with *May Wilson*," she said with a teasing smile.

"It's business, Kit; strictly business."

***

Steele arrived at the office of Mr. Hamilton and walked in the door. May Wilson had her back to him at a file cabinet, then turned around.

"Hello, may I... oh it's you, Mr. Reid." Her eyes narrowed. "Did you have an appointment today?"

Steele stepped further into the room. "No, I was in the area so I decided to stop by."

The edges of May's lips raised slightly, then fell back to her professional smile.

"Was there something you wanted?"

"Actually, it's the strangest thing, but I must have lost that brochure Mr. Hamilton gave me on trust funds. I still haven't gotten a chance to discuss this thoroughly with my sister, so I want to make sure I have that brochure with me when I do."

Miss Wilson walked over to a display table and took hold of one of the brochures.

She walked over and handed it to him. "Here's another one. We have many, so if for some reason you happen to lose it again, you know where to find me—I mean the brochures."

Steele's jaw lifted in that famous smile of his. The kind of smile that would say things to women without a word being spoken.

May pulled herself away from his gaze, then cleared her throat. "Would there be anything else, Mr. Reid?"

He pointed to one of the chairs. "Do you mind? I have a little bit of time to kill before I need to get back to work."

"No, I don't mind; have a seat. However, Mr. Hamilton is not here this morning if you had any further questions for him."

He directed that charming smile once more. "No, I would rather just sit and talk with you; if you don't mind."

May brushed her hand down the side of her neck. "That's fine, but I do have to continue with my work."

Steele casually glanced around the room when he noticed a bandana hanging on one of the hooks of a coatrack.

May took notice of his prolonged stare. "Is there a question, Mr. Reid?" she asked and glanced at the coatrack.

"No, I was just admiring that nice-looking bandana. Is that yours?"

"Yes, I wear it when it's a bit windy out to cover my hair."

Steele gazed at her. "You do have very beautiful hair."

May's cheekbones lifted with a smile. "Why thank you, Mr. Reid, that is very nice of you to say."

"You must have forgotten your bandana last week," he said in a probing voice.

Her eyes sharpened with an inquisitive stare. "I don't know what you mean?"

"At the Lakeside Country Club. I was there last week as a guest, and I saw you and the manager, Miss Thomas talking. It was windy that day, so that's why I said you must've forgotten your bandana."

Miss Wilson sat up straighter in her chair. "Why Mr. Reid, you are very observant as to notice I wasn't wearing my bandana. And yes, I was there at the country club talking with Miss Thomas." She glanced him over with a questioning stare. "And why didn't you make your presence known and say hello?"

"I saw you from a distance while I was talking to a man at the Pro shop. Besides, you appeared to be deep in conversation and I didn't want to interrupt you. Also, we had only met for a brief amount of time before, and I wasn't sure you would recognize me."

She glanced up from her work. "You're a hard man *not* to recognize Mr. Reid."

"Should I take that as a compliment?"

She attempted to suppress her smile. "Take it as you may, Mr. Reid; I'm just stating a fact."

"Very well, then I think *I will* take it as a compliment."

Miss Wilson held a pursed smile, then went back to her work.

Steele interjected again. "Tell me, how do you know Miss Thomas? Do you have a membership at the club? I only ask, because it seems to be a very prestigious club and people like you and me usually can't afford something like that."

"First of all, never presume anything—a lesson I have learned over the years. And two, Miss Thomas and I are friends, so I have an open invitation to visit her at the club anytime I like. And three, how *did you* get invited as a guest? Guests are there by invitation only when they are considering membership. You just said that people *like us* usually can't afford it."

Steele smiled to her wittiness. "Very good, Miss Wilson. And you're right, I can't afford something like that. I was invited by Mrs. Eve Hamilton, who in a strange coincidence, I just happened to meet the day after I was here the last time. And when a woman of her social status invites you, you don't turn something like that down. Honestly, I only went there so I could take my niece. She never gets to do more classy activities, so I thought she might like to get dressed up and enjoy the club for the day."

"I see. And did you and your niece enjoy the day?"

"Yes, very much. I'm not sure it's a place I would enjoy on a regular basis, but it was fine for that day. So, tell me; how long have you known Miss Thomas? I sat and talked with her a while and she seems like a nice person."

"Yes, she's a very nice person. We happened to meet at the courthouse. I was there on a personal matter, and she was there trying to help her brother with a legal issue."

"And what issue might that be? I only ask, because when we were talking, Mr. Hamilton happened to pass by our table and stopped to say hello. After he left, I asked her if she knew him well. She then commented that there were two sides to him. I asked her to elaborate on that, and that's when she opened up and told me that Mr. Hamilton had treated her brother badly. She then asked me to please keep what she told me in confidence—which I did."

"Well, first of all, she shouldn't have made that comment to you. And yes, that's how we became friends. You see, while we were both waiting outside our prospective courtrooms, she began to tell me about the matter her brother was having against Mr. Hamilton and his law firm. I won't go into details, but I do understand both sides as I now work for the law firm myself. However, after her brother lost in trying to obtain this certain property, Mr. Hamilton's investment firm did something that to me was a conflict of interest. Anyway, that's why Darlene is so bitter about it, as it ruined her brother's construction business. He is just barely beginning to put the pieces back together in his life."

"I see. I could tell it bothers her very much."

"Yes, it does. And it's understandable that she would feel that way. Maybe one day soon Darlene will be able to get resolution and put this whole thing behind her."

"And you, Miss Wilson? How do you feel about him? I only ask, because if I deal with this law firm, I want to make sure the person behind it is on the up-and-up."

"Oh, you don't have to worry about that, this law firm is definitely on the up-and-up. And as far as Mr. Hamilton, there are things which I know he does, like giving to charities, which I admire. And besides, the part that I had a problem with, was not this law firm. It was an investment company to which Mr. Hamilton has stock. Now that isn't to say he doesn't have his; well let's just say, his particular ways."

Steele narrowed his brow. "His particular ways? I don't know what you mean."

"Mr. Hamilton is very particular about every little detail. Did you happen to notice his office, how everything was so neatly in its place?"

"Yes, as a matter of fact, I did. It was very neat, and when I walked up to that display case of that vintage gun on the credenza, he quickly stopped me from placing my hands on it. Apparently, he didn't want any smudge marks on the glass."

"Yes, and he is like that with every aspect of his life. There was one time recently when we were at his vacation home in Southport. I had to go with him because it was a work-related meeting he was having. We walked over to his study and he unlocked the door. He took a few steps into the room, then looked around. I could tell by the look on his face that something wasn't quite right. He then looked to the back of the room and pointed to one of the chairs sitting on a rug. These chairs are perfectly set at corner angles in front of the gun case. This gun case is very large and sits on the rug in front of a large wall of bookcases. These two chairs are vintage French Regency mahogany fireside chairs. Now, these chairs no one is to sit in them, they are just for show. Anyway, when we walked into the room, he pointed to the chair on the left and tells me, 'That's strange, that chair is out of place. I know for a fact the last time I was in here; everything was in its place.' He then walked over and looked down at the feet of the chair. He then said, 'See, I was right, it *has been* moved. Do you see those little indentations in the rug? The front feet of the chair should be exactly set in that groove. Both the cleaning maid knows this and so does Poppy. He then glanced at the wall of bookcases with a pensive look on his face, then he said, 'I will have to speak to Poppy and the maid about this.' He then meticulously moved the chair so that the feet of the chair set perfectly in the grooves on the rug."

Steele shook his head. "I can't imagine being that particular about the location of a couple of chairs. But maybe this behavior stems from something he opened up to me about. He told me that when he was young, his family was very poor. And at a point in his life, he vowed to never be poor again. Therefore, my theory is, that because of his poverty growing up he is now very guarded with things he possesses in life—like those chairs."

A look of surprise rose on May's face. "Why Mr. Reid, that is an amazing conclusion you have drawn for not knowing him very well. In all the time I've known him, I have never made that connection. But you are right; that's probably why he is so particular about everything he owns."

Steele glanced at the clock. "Well, it's been a pleasure talking with you, but I better be on my way. I have a full day ahead of me and I need to pick up my niece."

Miss Wilson lowered her brow. "Doesn't your niece have school during the day?"

"She is on summer vacation from her school."

"Oh, yes, that's right."

Steele stood to his feet. "It was so nice seeing you again, Miss Wilson. You are a pleasure to talk to."

"You also, Mr. Reid. But seeing how we have gotten to know each other on a different level today; you can call me May."

Steele smiled. "May, such a pretty name. Thank you, May. And you can call me Jeffrey."

Her cheeks lifted with a warm smile. "Good day, Jeffrey."

"Good day, Miss May."

***

Steele drove towards the country club to pick up Kit. What Kit had teased him about the other day, had begun to manifest itself between him and May Wilson. Steele hadn't had genuine feelings for someone since his wife Rachel. And the thought of pursuing those types of feelings again, caused a warm sensation to lay upon his heart. But thinking on this, there arose in him a dilemma. He had to keep his feelings in check and his mind clear. After all, she was one of the subjects in a possible murder conspiracy, therefore he had to keep his objectivity.

As he drove into the parking area, Kit was there at the curb. She got into his car with a picked flower in her hand.

"What's that?" he said glancing at the flower.

"You're not going to believe it, but one of those preppy-looking boys gave it to me. I was just sitting there waiting to see if Miss Thomas and Mr. Hamilton were going to talk when this boy sat down in the chair beside me. He introduced himself as Tom, and then gave me the flower. He said the way I look in my flowery dress, made him think of picking this flower and giving it to me. He then smiled and said he hoped to see more of me at the club. You know me, usually I would have something sarcastic to say. But I was so flabbergasted by the whole thing, not a single word came out of my mouth. But why would he do something like that? He doesn't know me."

Steele started the car and began to drive off the club grounds. "Kit your fifteen years old now. You mean to tell me after getting dressed up, doing your hair, and looking into your mirror, that you didn't think you looked pretty?"

"I don't know, I guess I look okay."

"No, not okay, you look very pretty; and apparently that boy thought so too. Enough for him to take a chance on you rejecting his gift, to make an impression on you. Get used to it kiddo, it's going to start to happen more and more."

Kit sat in silence thinking about that for a moment. Finally, she spoke up. "Oh, by the way, Mr. Hamilton and Miss Thomas did talk to each other."

"And were you able to listen in on their conversation?"

"Yes, because they sat at the table across from mine. Mr. Hamilton first said his pleasantries to her, but she was not very open and friendly."

"How do you mean?"

"He tried to get her to sit down and talk with him, but she kept saying she needed to get back to work. I did however hear one important thing. Mr. Hamilton asked her if she was going to Southport and be there at his birthday event along with May. Miss Thomas then asked when the party was, and he said next Sunday. He said he would be there on Saturday along with Poppy, as she was going to be there getting ready for the event. Miss Thomas then said she would try to make it, but she wasn't sure. Mr. Hamilton then told her that if she goes, to also invite her brother, Daniel to come. He said he wants to sit down with him and talk things out to let bygones be bygones. When he said that about the brother, it seemed to irritate Miss Thomas. She then turned and said abruptly, I'll try, and then she walked off."

"A lot to interpret in that little conversation. It sounded like Miss Thomas didn't want to talk much, maybe because she felt guilty of what she might be planning against him. I'm glad you were there listening because now we know about the party that is planned for Mr. Hamilton's birthday. Also, that he and Poppy will be there on Saturday. If the two women are going to try something against him, Saturday would be the perfect time to do it with no other guests around. And since Poppy will be there on Saturday, maybe she is the one who is going to let Miss Thomas and May into the house. Remember, Poppy has keys to everything."

Kit interjected. "So, are we going to be there on Saturday in case that's when they plan on trying something against Mr. Hamilton?"

"Yes and no. Meaning, not you. Remember, when I go to Southport, I will be going with Eve Hamilton for the purpose of catching her husband in an affair. It wouldn't make sense for you to go with me if we are only trying to catch him in the act. But in the meantime, I need to talk to her. I want her to be the one to tell me about the upcoming party. I want to see if she suggests herself that we go out there on Saturday. She will probably think this is the best opportunity to catch her husband with Poppy, with no other guests around. Remember, even though we are looking at the possibility of the conspiracy to kill Mr. Hamilton, I still need Eve to think this is only about catching her husband in the affair."

Kit nodded her head. "Yes, you're right. So, what are you going to do if you catch Miss Wilson or Miss Thomas or the brother, attempting to kill him?"

"I do have a registered gun as a PI, so I will pull it out if necessary. But as far as alerting the local police to a possible shooting, I've changed my mind. Look, if we are entirely wrong about this conspiracy to kill Mr. Hamilton, then how am I going to explain why I called out the local police? However, I may go to the Southport Police Station and feel things out. I want to see what kind of cooperation they will give me in the event something happens. But for now, I think I'm going to have to play this one by ear. I'll play things out with Eve of spying on her husband at the house and go from there."

"Well, just be careful. We do know those two women talked of getting a gun, so that part of this is very real."

"I hear what you're saying. And yes, I'll be very careful." Steele then turned towards the front door. "Hey, I think I hear someone coming up the steps. By the heavy-sounding boot, I think it's Jake."

Kit quickly went over to the file cabinet to act busy. Jake gave a courtesy knock then opened the door and took a step inside.

He looked at Steele. "Afternoon, Mr. Steele."

His eyes then drifted to the girl standing by the file cabinet. Upon focusing, his eyes grew large and he shook his head in a double-take. "Wowie Kazowie! Is that you, Kit?"

She turned and brushed her hand down the length of her dress. "Yeah, it's me. Why are you just staring with your eyes bugged out? Never seen a girl in a dress before?"

"Sure, it's just that you look so, like wow, really pretty."

Kit walked over to him and placed her hands on her hips. "And what are you saying, Jake? That I have to wear a dress to be pretty?"

"No, it's just that I've never seen you all dressed up before. Besides, I've always known you were pretty even in your regular clothes." Jake shyly looked down and scuffed his shoe against the floor. "I mean come on Kit; you don't think I bring you guys a newspaper during the week for nothing, do ya?"

Kit glanced at Steele with a conceding look on her face. He was right about Jake liking her.

Jake nervously scuffed his shoe against the floor once more. "You know, there's a town hall dance coming up soon. I was wondering..."

Her eyes grew wide. "You were wondering what?"

"I was wondering if you might like to go with me? You could wear that pretty dress and all."

Kit looked at Steele like a caged animal looking for a way out.

She took a step back. "Well, I don't know. I'm really not into going to dances and all that."

The hopeful look on Jake's face sunk like a rock. It was all he could do to hold back his emotions.

"I understand. I guess you wouldn't be into something like that. I just thought I would ask."

Kit glanced at Steele who directed a stern look not to hurt his feelings. She looked at Jake who had disappointment draped all over his face.

"Okay," she added. "Let me think about it. But first I'll need to ask permission from my foster parents if I can go."

Jake's face lit up with excitement. "Really? That's so great! Yeah, ask your foster parents. And if you like, tell your foster parents that my mom will drive us there. Or if you prefer, maybe Mr. Steele would want to drive you and you can meet me there."

She glanced at Steele, who nodded his approval.

"Yes, maybe that's better if Rick drives me and I'll meet you there."

Jake glanced at the clock. "I guess I better get going." He walked towards the door when he turned back. "Oh, I almost forgot the newspaper." He reached out and handed her the paper. "Thanks again, Kit. Even if you don't want to dance, I know it will be fun just being with you."

She smiled. "Okay, Jake, and thanks for asking."

"No problem; see you later."

When Jake closed the door, she turned to Steele. "Okay, you were right again, *he is* sweet on me."

"This is a good thing, Kit. Jake's a nice young man."

"Yeah, I guess. But now I'm going to have to learn how to dance. But there's no way I'm going to try any of those swing dances the kids are doing. Maybe just a slow dance or two."

"Why don't you ask your foster mother to help you. I think she might like that."

"You think?" She glanced to the side. "Yeah, maybe you're right. I'll ask Carol to help me." She redirected her focus. "And what about you, Rick?"

He furrowed his brow. "What about me?"

"I'm sure at Mr. Hamilton's birthday party there will be dancing. You should ask May Wilson to dance?"

Steele walked towards the window and looked down onto the street. Then he turned with a contemplative look resting upon his face.

"Yeah, I'm not sure how that would work. I mean, picture this... I walk up to May and say, 'Would you like to dance? And by the way, do you and Miss Thomas plan on shooting Mr. Hamilton?' Yeah, that should go over well."

Kit chuckled. "Yes, I see your point. But like you said about this case; it has many twists and turns. Maybe there will be a new twist which will come up and you will find out that May and Miss Thomas are not trying to kill Mr. Hamilton after all."

Steele directed an unknowing look. "I certainly hope so."

Chapter Eight

Monday of the next week, Steele called the home of Eve Hamilton and hung up after one ring. About ten minutes later, she returned the call and they agree to meet at his office.

When Eve arrived, they greeted each other and sat down at his desk.

"Tell me, Mr. Steele, any progress in finding out which of these women might be having the affair with my husband?"

Steele knowing what he knew about May Wilson and Miss Thomas obtaining a gun, thought to be careful how to answer.

"In regards to Darlene, I used my investigative techniques to try to get information. I went to the Lakeside Country Club where I used a false identity to gather more information. I even spoke to Miss Thomas face-to-face where I casually brought up the subject of your husband. She mentioned that she knew him and thought well of him, but there were two sides to him."

"Oh really? And what side was she talking about? His romantic bedside manner side?"

"No, I didn't gather she had any feelings for him other than a friendly acquaintance. I can usually pick up if a person has any kind of romantic feelings for someone. But when I brought up his name, her immediate reaction and facial expression showed none of that. In fact, it was quite the opposite."

Eve sharpened her focus. "What do you mean, by opposite?"

"She brought up the subject of her brother's issues with Mr. Hamilton."

"Oh yes, I know of that situation. I believe her brother wanted to purchase a block of buildings to invest in, and my husband's law firm represented another party who had an interest in it as well. Some issues about building codes."

"Yes, and Darlene seemed genuinely bitter about it. She seemed very torn between the two feelings she had about him. Bitter about what happened to her brother, but at the same time, she seemed to admire him in other ways."

"Maybe that admiration is the affair she is having with him."

Steele held a contemplative stare. "My gut feeling is telling me it's not her."

"Maybe your gut is wrong this time."

"Perhaps; but the last time my gut was wrong about an investigation, was when I first started on the police force. I had multiple suspects in a murder case and I zeroed in on a particular suspect based on the prevailing evidence. However, I made the mistake of getting tunnel vision and only looked at the evidence of that one individual. It turned out to be someone I never suspected."

"Well, speaking of other suspects, what about Miss Wilson, his secretary?"

"Yes, May Wilson. I have spoken with her twice at length. And both times I did not sense she was having an affair with him either. Yes, she does admire him very much, but only professionally. She did mention something about there being two sides to every person, so she must have seen another side of him. I also gathered that she has higher aspirations other than being a secretary. I noticed a few books on her desk that deal with being a contract lawyer. Honestly, I think she sees your husband as more of a mentor than anything."

Eve slightly frowned, then seemed to shake it off. "Then it's probably the person I suspected most in the first place; it's Poppy. When my husband is away in Southport, she is with him a lot of the time he is there. When they are working together, I'm sure they take time out for their *romantic interludes*."

Steele thought to use this opening to fill in the blanks about Poppy.

"Yes, you mentioned your husband spending a lot of time with her. Now you said as a property manager, that she has access to the house in Southport?"

"Yes, she has keys to all the doors."

"What about the door to his study? You mentioned before that he always has it locked when he's not there."

"Just recently he gave Poppy a key to that door also. He said he wanted her to have access in the event he wants her to pre-pare the room if he is having guests; like his old college buddies. I found it a bit concerning that he views Poppy on the same level as me, to give her a key to his precious study. He practically con-siders it his sanctuary. Anyway, enough about keys. Tell me, Mr. Steele, are you ready for our trip to Southport?"

"Sure, but when do you want to go? Did you find out when the next time he is going to be there?"

"Yes, he has his 40th birthday coming up this weekend. He will be there starting on Saturday, but his birthday event will be on Sunday. However, he told me not to go there on Saturday as he has some work to do, plus Poppy would be busy setting things up for his birthday. This makes me feel he doesn't want me there on Saturday so he can spend his romantic time with her. But this is when we need to catch him."

"And how do you plan on catching him? I know you told me to make sure I have my camera, but we can't just waltz in through the front door. We need to catch them in some kind of romantic interaction."

"Don't worry, I have it all figured out. I will give you more details on our three-hour drive over there, but here are the ba-sics. We will check into the hotel and settle into our rooms and then get some rest from the drive. Then have a light afternoon meal, and then around 5:30 pm, we will drive over to the house. My husband is a stickler on his schedule, so even when he isn't conducting business, he is always in his study working on something until exactly six o'clock. If I didn't mention it before, my husband is a perfectionist to a fault. He wants everything in a certain order and everything on a schedule." Eve half laughed. "He probably even tells Poppy how much time they have to be in bed together down to the very minute."

"Yes, May Wilson told me he has to have everything in its proper place."

"Especially in that sacred study of his. That is why I want to be there before six o'clock because I know he will still be in that study. When it gets near that hour, Poppy will probably come into the study to help him straighten up. While they are doing that, he will probably switch from his business demeanor to showing her some affection. This is when you will be ready to take photos of them. It will not be dark yet, so I don't think you will need a flashbulb. I have keys to the side gate which cannot be seen from the front of the house in case Poppy happens to be in the formal living room. My husband's study is in the east wing on the first floor. You will have to navigate over a small retaining wall and over to a patio where there are French doors. Stay hidden against the house until you get to the doors. The curtains are drawn to the side of those doors, so that should help block them from seeing you. Once you peek around and see them in any physical contact, move to the front of the door and take as many photos as you can; including Poppy running from the scene. In the meantime, I would have quietly gone into the house through the front door and wait near the bottom of the stairs where I can stay hidden. If I know Poppy, she will be so embarrassed by the whole thing, she will try to run out of the house. I would have already locked the front door with the key, so she will not be able to get out. Then I will confront her about having an affair with my husband. In the meantime, you quickly climb back over the wall and come to the front door where I will let you in."

"And you don't think Randall will get violent? I mean, he does have a collection of guns."

"He is not the violent type. He does have that collection, but they are only for show. He takes people down by filing legal actions, not pulling a trigger. But don't worry, he won't be able to file any action against you for trespassing or invasion of privacy, because I would have given you permission. In fact, on the day we leave for Southport, I will have something in writing that says I have given you full access to the house to take any photos in the course of your investigation. With Randall, you have to cover all of your bases."

"What if I don't see them in any romantic embrace to take photos while they are there in the study?"

"Then come back to the front of the house. There are windows on either side of the front door, so motion with your hand that you were unable to get the photos. I will wait hidden to see if my husband and Poppy will go upstairs and into the bedroom. I will then unlock the front door and let you in. Then make your way up the stairs to the master bedroom which is the furthest door on the west wing, which is left of the staircase. Then burst into the room and hopefully catch them in the act."

"Now just to be sure, nobody else should be there on Saturday?"

"No, there shouldn't be. Everyone who is invited to his birthday event will come on Sunday."

"I was just curious; are Miss Wilson and Miss Thomas invited to his birthday event?"

"Yes, Randall placed them on the list of guests. Since we decided to do this event at the last minute, we did not request RSVPs. But to answer your question, yes, both of them were invited. I believe Miss Thomas' brother, Daniel, was invited also. I think my husband wishes to bury the hatchet with her brother. In business, he can be a shark, but in his personal life, he wants everyone to like him with nothing hanging over his head. But if you ask me, I don't think the brother is interested to bury any hatchet. Honestly, I think he would rather bury the hatchet into my husband's chest."

"Really? He hates him that much?"

"Randall ruined his life. My husband's obsession with winning and controlling everything with his money makes him many enemies, and a resentful wife."

"I do have a question about Poppy. You said that she is married, correct?"

"Yes, she is."

"Tell me; if she spends so much time with your husband, doesn't Poppy's husband get upset by that?"

"I am glad you brought that up. Because that is one aspect that could come up as Poppy's husband is a very jealous man. Maybe his jealousy started because she spends so much time with Randall, or he is just like that. There have been several incidents where he has come to the Southport house to confront them. The husband, Ralph Sorenson, drinks a lot and when he gets drunk, he gets enraged if Poppy spends too much time alone with Randall. One time we had a gathering when Ralph drove up to the house and burst in the front door yelling at the top of his voice. Poppy then pulled him outside where he was accusing her of sleeping with Randall. Poppy was able to calm him down to a point, with the husband saying a few obscenities, then he drove off in his truck. Poppy apologized for his behavior, but I know they have seen professional counseling in the past about their marital problems."

"Thanks, that's good information to know. Now, how are we going to do this? Do I drive my car, you drive yours, or we go in separate cars?"

"If nothing happens in regards to catching them together, then Randall will expect me to be arriving in my car. And if that happens, I'll just tell him that I invited you to come along to rub elbows with some of the guests—you being Mr. Reid, of course. If he asks, just say you work for an investment firm. That we met when I went to your office to seek advice on possible future investments."

"Yes, that's a good cover story for how we met."

"As I said before Mr. Steele, I have everything covered. Now on Saturday, I'll pick you up here at the office around ten o'clock. That will give us plenty of time to drive down there and then check into the hotel. Then when it gets close to the time, we will drive to the house and try to catch him with her."

Steele interjected. "And if it's not Poppy that he's having an affair with?"

"Then I will just have to proceed with the divorce without the evidence of infidelity. What I will do, is claim spousal neglect of him not performing his husbandly duties, due to the fact of his suspected affairs with other women. When neither Randall nor Poppy can deny they spend hours and hours together alone on the weekends, the judge will only be able to conclude that the preponderance of evidence backs up my claim."

Steele raised his brow. "I'm impressed. You seem to know a lot about law and law terminology."

"When you are around a lawyer as much as I have been the past few years, you learn a thing or two. But getting back to the divorce proceedings; I don't think Randall will contest it. The battle will be on how much money he is willing to part with, and what the court will award me."

Steele rose to his feet. "Very well; I will see you on Saturday morning around ten."

"Yes, and I will have you sign that paper that says you have permission to enter the premises at Southport."

"Sounds like you have it all figured out and your bases covered."

Eve held a pensive look in her eye. "Yes, I do—not a stone left unturned."

As Steele watched Eve Hamilton walk out the door, he thought about the coming events. Eve seemed to have everything well thought out; maybe too much for his liking. However, there was a big variable in this plan that could change everything. If Miss Wilson, Miss Thomas, and Daniel were planning something against Mr. Hamilton, they would have to do it on Saturday. If this occurs, then they would all be there at the same time that Steele and Eve would be spying on Randall and Poppy. And if that transpires, then the feeling he had been having in his gut was right. This ship, like the Titanic, was heading into icy waters. And the icebergs coming his way were getting more ominous by the minute.

Chapter Nine

Eve Hamilton arrived at ten o'clock and entered the office. As Steele gathered his belongings, including his camera, he turned to Kit.

"Well Kit, I'll be leaving now. Do you think you can handle being in the office by yourself all day?"

She rolled her eyes. "I know how to run this office like the back of my hand. If a new client comes in, I'll take thorough notes on why they need our services and set up an appointment for next week. We no longer take cases of missing dogs or cats, and your fees are eight dollars a day plus expenses."

He smiled. "Very good, I know the office is in good hands."

She waved. "Have a good trip, and watch out for those roller coaster rides," she said with a telling look.

He nodded his head. "I definitely will."

The two walked down the steps, and over to Eve's car. He tossed his briefcase and a small travel bag in the back and got in the front seat.

As they got on their way, Eve opened the conversation. "Tell me, what was that thing between you and Kit about roller coasters?"

"Oh, it's just something we say when a case has a lot of twists and turns."

Eve glanced at Steele with a pondering stare. "And why would she say that about *this case*? As far as I'm concerned, there haven't been any interesting twists at all."

Steele thought about what he and Kit knew about Miss Wilson and Miss Thomas and their possible conspiracy against Mr. Hamilton.

"Yes, so far nothing has happened. But based upon other cases, we know things can change on a dime."

For the next hour, they made small talk and commented about the scenic drive.

Eve glanced at Steele then back to the road. "You know, when we first met that night in your office, I brought up the subject of that unopened bottle of bourbon on your shelf. Kit was very vague about the reasons why you have it there, and all you said was it's a reminder not to drink. You also said you might tell me the whole story if you felt our relationship would progress to a certain point." She glanced his way once more. "So, has it progressed to that point?"

Steele sat silent as he pondered the question. Finally, he spoke up. "Alright, I guess it has reached that point to tell you the whole story. I had just been promoted to an investigator in the police force. One day I went into the Woolworths to pick up a new can opener when I turned a corner and accidentally ran into this woman. When our eyes met, it was like I truly breathed for the first time. I said my apologies and then we introduced ourselves. She told me her name was Rachel, and she had just moved into town. There was something so special about her, that I just had to ask her for dinner. Everything was so perfect. I know everyone says that, but I knew I had found the person I wanted to spend the rest of my life with. It was a whirlwind romance as they say, and we were married about six months later. Every day was something new as we were building a future together. One evening I had gone to bed early, as I had worked a double shift. We lived in a two-story house, so Rachel was downstairs probably reading a book, as she loved to read. Suddenly, I woke up to her screaming. It was as if she was being muffled as she tried to scream and call out my name. As I rushed to get out of bed, I heard scuffling noises and the front door seemed to bang against the wall. I ran downstairs calling out her name, then I looked outside to see her being placed into the back of a dark sedan. It seemed at that point like she had been knocked out as her body was limp. By the time I ran towards the street, the car had sped off. Immediately I called the station and they put out an all-points bulletin. As I and my fellow officers searched the streets and local highways, my mind was in a panic. The sergeant suggested I go home and wait just in case this was a kidnapping and they would call for a ransom. While I was at my home, I searched my house for any clues. I saw that Rachel was apparently reading, as the light on the end table was on and her book had been set face down to the page she was reading. This led me to believe that she must have heard a knock on the door and when she went to answer it, that's when the person abducted her. I searched for clues, but the only thing I saw was a small scuff mark on the entry tile. I know it wasn't mine because it was brown polish and I only wear black soled shoes. As time when on, any leads of finding the dark sedan all came to dead ends. Now, there was a theory I had as to why she was abducted. I had just started to work on a case where I suspected possible corruption of some fellow police officers in the department. I was investigating a string of robberies where I felt that some officers were being paid to look the other way. My theory was that I was getting too close to the investigation and they abducted Rachel as a warning to back off. I fully expected to get a note or a back-alley warning, to stop looking into those officers, and in turn, my wife would be released. But months went by with nothing; not a word. All trails seemed to disappear on her whereabouts and my hope of finding her grew dimmer every day. Then around nine months later, a highway patrol officer was going to have lunch so he pulled into a dirt road where people throw a lot of trash and a few abandoned cars. That's when he noticed that one of the cars had recently been burned up. He went to take a look and found there was a burned body in the car. The coroner said it was a woman about Rachel's height, and he estimated the age by tooth remains to be in her mid-twenties; which would match Rachel's age. However, he said it was hard to positively identify the body because it was badly burned. Since it was only around thirty miles from where we lived and she was never seen again, we assumed it must have been her. The remains of her body were buried at the Hillsdale Cemetery." Steele looked off to the side in remembrance. "There were times when it was as if I could feel her telling me it's okay and to go on with my life. But the thing is, it wasn't okay. I loved her so much and I was so lost without her in my life. Then between the corruption I suspected in the department and losing my wife, I began to drink more and more. Soon I was even coming into my shift drunk and I began to get into fights with everyone, including my superior officer. At first, I was suspended, and finally, I was let go from the force."

Eve glanced his way, then back to the road. "I'm so sorry. That must have been horrible for you to lose your wife that way."

"Thank you, it was a very rough time in my life. Then because I had lost my job, I lost my house to foreclosure. Then before I knew it, I was basically a drunk out on the streets. I would scrounge around for soda pop and beer bottles and cash them in for the redemption. Then I would turn around and buy another bottle of cheap booze. This went on for about two years where I lost all hope and blamed God for taking away my wife. Then one day I was in the back of a market looking for bottles when I saw a young girl around thirteen years old doing the same. At first, I got mad and tried to shoo her way, saying this was my spot. Then she said something to me that I will never forget. She said, 'I live in a foster home where they treat me very badly because I'm not their real daughter. They don't feed me enough food, so I have to find bottles to cash in just to eat enough. I was born at the end of The Great Depression, where both my parents contracted tuberculosis and died. At first, I was sent to an orphanage and from there, it was one foster home after another. Now that's my story, mister; but what's your excuse? You are an able-bodied young man who can go out and get a real job, so you have no excuses. Why don't you get off your sorry butt and do something with your life! When I turn eighteen, I'm going out on my own and make something of myself!'

Her words hit me like a ton of bricks, and it was as if those words sobered me out of my drunken stupor. Then this girl's attitude suddenly changed from chewing me out to one of compassion. She took me by the hand and started walking somewhere. I asked her where we were going, and she said to church. She said she goes to this church once a week to pray. She said she prays to God that she will never feel hatred in her heart to those who have treated her badly. She went on to say, if Jesus on the cross could say, 'forgive them because they know not what they do', that she herself could find it in her heart to forgive the people who have hurt her too.' Her words pierced my heart and we walked into that church and knelt at a pew as she silently prayed. With my emotions flooding my heart, I said this prayer. 'God, if you are truly out there, then I want the same thing that this young girl has. I want to be able to forgive those who have hurt me, and I want to begin to live my life again.' In that instant, I felt as though a hand reached out and took the burdens off of me. And from that moment on, I stopped drinking with none of the shakes from the booze." Steele glanced towards Eve. "And that's why I keep that bottle on the shelf. It's a reminder of how low I had gotten in my life, and how I don't ever want to go there again."

"That thirteen-year-old girl that helped you out; do you ever see her anymore?"

Steele smiled. "Yes, we just saw her about an hour ago—it was Kit."

Eve nodded in acknowledgment. "And that's why a thirty-two-year-old man and a fifteen-year-old girl become such close friends?"

"Yes, probably as close as two friends can be."

Steele decided to lay his head on the back of the seat. He pretended to be sleeping, but his mind was traveling a mile-a-minute. The investigation had been deafly quiet up until this point and time. But as he tried to make sense of it all, he had a strange feeling this whole thing was going to blow up.

Eve abruptly came to a stop which alerted Steele. He had apparently fallen asleep the last leg of their journey. He looked up to see they had reached their destination and sat up in his seat. As he helped Eve with her overnight bag, they walked into the grand foyer of the hotel. A hotel room in this place, he thought, would cost him a month's salary.

Eve approached the concierge at the front counter. Steele thought it interesting how they treated her like royalty, yet treated him as a commoner. When they arrived at their rooms which were next to each other, Eve turned to him.

"It's a little after two right now. Why don't we meet back here in the hallway around 5:30? It takes only fifteen minutes to get out to the coastal road where the house is located. I'm going to take a nap from the long drive, then take a shower, and have a light meal before we leave. Since you apparently have already taken a nap, you do, well, whatever it is you do."

"Actually, I might go for a walk. I saw they have a museum a couple of blocks from here. Walking helps me think."

"Very well, we'll meet right here at 5:30."

As Eve shut the door to her room, Steele entered his room, unpacked a few toiletry items, and headed back out. He only told Eve he was going to the museum, but instead, he was going to take a cab over to the Southport police station. He wanted to see if he felt he could trust anyone there and to see what kind of support he could expect if he needed to call on them.

The cab driver pulled to the curb, as Steele exited and made his way into the Southport Police Station. After identifying himself as a private investigator, the sergeant in charge seemed to take to him. As they spent some time talking, he mentioned the case he was working on which brought him to Southport. He asked Sergeant McMurphy if things went south in the investigation if he could count on their assistance if necessary. Sergeant McMurphy offered Steele any assistance he needed.

Steele arrived back at the hotel just in time to freshen up. A few minutes later he met Eve in the hallway.

She placed her purse around her shoulder. "Tell me, Mr. Steele, are you ready for what we have planned this evening?"

"Yes, I have my camera in my shoulder strap, and a piece for protection in my ankle holster."

Eve eyed him with caution. "You say you have a piece; as in a gun?"

"Yes, on this type of investigation where I will be accessing someone's personal property, it's best if I'm prepared for anything. I know you said your husband only *collects guns*, but if he felt a burglar was seeking to do harm, wouldn't he defend himself and his loved ones?"

She stared down at the concealed weapon in his lower leg. "You won't pull out your gun unless you have to, right? I don't want any accidents."

"You can rest easy; I know how and when to use my firearm."

They got in her car and began driving to the house. The view was incredible as they approached the scenic coast. Steele thought that perhaps one day he would like to visit this area, under different circumstances of course. As they drove closer, he could feel the core of his body tense. This was not like him to feel this nervous conducting an investigation. Perhaps that famous gut of his was delivering a warning. His mind then drifted to the night his wife Rachel was abducted. If he only had his firearm by his side that night, maybe things would have been different.

Eve turned down a street that was lined with mansions with expansive ocean views—only for the rich with deep pockets. A thought flashed in his mind; how this street full of mansions was a far cry from when he used to live at The Alley.

"It's right up there," she said, breaking his thoughts. "It's the house on the left with ivy growing up the walls. I'll park just a bit past the entrance behind the hedges so Randall or Poppy won't see my car."

As Eve had stated, the sun had not yet dipped below the horizon. Steele took hold of his camera and placed the strap over his shoulder. He bent down and adjusted his ankle holster—just in case.

Eve pointed to the right. "We need to walk around the side of the property and up to the east gate. I'll unlock the gate and then there is a short walk until we get to block wall. Once we are there, I'll tell you where you need to scale the wall that separates the front and back yards. It's not that tall, only about four feet."

"You don't have a dog, do you? I don't want to run into a German Shepard."

"No, I always wanted a cat for our house in Charlotte. But Randall has one of those allergies where he coughs and sneezes when he gets near dogs or cats—it's something about their fur."

As they walked closer to the house, Eve held her finger to her lips for them to remain silent. She stooped down as they began to walk along the four-foot wall that separates the front and back yards. She then slowly lifted her head and peered over the wall, then ducked back down.

"I see them. They're in the study as I thought. If you look closely, you can barely see Randall sitting at his desk. I saw Poppy walk up to him, then she walked back out of view." Eve filled her lungs with a nervous breath. "Okay, it's time. Are you ready?"

"Yes. Now just to reiterate; you are going to quietly go in through the front door and wait hidden behind the staircase. Are you sure they won't hear you come in?"

"Do you see how big this house is? The east wing is down this long hallway and then you turn left up another hallway. Then his study is in the back of this seven-thousand square foot house. They won't hear me unless Poppy happens to pass the formal living room on her way to the kitchen for something. But I don't think she will, because as I said, she will go into the study to help him clean up at exactly six o'clock."

Steele looked at his watch. "Okay, it's a few minutes before the top of the hour. I'm going to start making my way over to the French doors. Hopefully, everything will go smoothly."

Eve took in another breath. "Yes, hopefully, it will."

Steele peered over the wall to make sure that neither Mr. Hamilton nor Poppy was within line of sight of seeing him scale the wall. He placed both hands on top of the wall and quickly lifted himself over. He rushed over and stood with his back against the stucco of the house. As he edged closer, he could feel himself breathe heavier from the anticipation of what was to come. He stepped onto the patio pavers and inched his way to the edge of the French doors. He glanced at his watch, which said two minutes until six o'clock. He peered in, using the drawn curtains as a shield, just as Eve had told him. As he waited, he saw Poppy enter the room and walk over to where Mr. Hamilton was sitting at his desk. Mr. Hamilton enclosed some papers into a folder and handed them to Poppy. She then walked over to a file cabinet and filtered through the drawer, then placed the file inside. Mr. Hamilton said something to her, which Steele could not make out what he had said. Poppy then walked over to his side, just as the chime of the standing grandfather clock struck the six o'clock hour. The two smiled at one another and it appeared that they might move in for a kiss or embrace. Steele pulled his camera to eye level and waited for the precise moment of their secret affection. Mr. Hamilton then lowered his gaze and pointed to a page from a magazine that made Poppy laugh. She then walked over to one side of the bookcase and took hold of a feather duster and proceeded to dust off the glass gun case. Seeing how they moved away from each other, Steele lowered the camera from eye level and relaxed his shoulders. Suddenly, the room became darker! Steele peered in and noticed that all the lights in the room had gone out. Due to the French doors being the only outside light, the room was now fairly dark. Mr. Hamilton then rose from his desk and said aloud, 'the power must be out.' Poppy then said she would try to reset the electric box in the back patio. She then left out the door, as Mr. Hamilton stood in the middle of the room waiting to see if the lights would come back on.

Without warning, a gunshot broke the silence! Steele reacted by checking his chest to see if he had been hit. He peered into the room to see Mr. Hamilton buckle over in pain as he fell to the floor! Steele drew his weapon from his ankle holster then kicked the French doors open and burst into the room! He quickly scanned the room with his gun in hand. Seeing no one was in the room, he placed it back in his holster. He then rushed to Mr. Hamilton's side and could see blood near his chest seeping into his dress shirt.

He heard Poppy cry out in the distance. "Mr. Hamilton! What was that! Was that a gunshot?"

A few moments later, Steele could hear the rushing of footsteps in the hallway back towards the study.

Steele had dealt with people being shot when he was on the force, so he knew to keep pressure on the wound. He cradled Mr. Hamilton in one arm and held his hand against the injured site.

Mr. Hamilton opened his eyes and looked up at Steele. "Chair," he said in a weakened voice.

"What about the chair?" asked Steele.

"Chair moved," he said, as his eyes rolled back and he fell unconscious.

Poppy then rushed into the room to see Mr. Hamilton bleeding and being held by Steele.

She cried out, "Mr. Hamilton!" Her eyes focused on the man holding him. "Who are you? And why are you in here?"

"Quick!" said Steele. "Get me a towel or something so I can put pressure on the wound!"

Poppy's entire body was shaking—she was frozen in a state of shock.

"Now, Poppy!" he yelled stronger. "Get me a towel!"

Poppy's eyes became clearer. She ran over to the wet bar which had a towel in one of the storage shelves.

"Here," she said and handed him the towel. "Is he going to be alright?"

"I don't know. Go to a telephone and call the Southport Police Department. Tell them you need a squad car and an ambulance. Also, tell them that Mr. Steele is requesting to have Sergeant McMurphy come out to the scene."

Poppy rushed over to the phone which was also under the wet bar. Suddenly Eve Hamilton came rushing into the room and out of breath.

She looked down at her husband. "Oh my goodness! What happened? Is he shot?"

Steele looked up. "Yes, he's been shot."

A minute later, several people came rushing into the room. It was Miss Wilson and Miss Thomas. Then a moment after that another man, he presumed was Miss Thomas' brother, came into the room also.

Steele addressed the whole group. "Someone, come quick and put pressure on this wound!"

The first to move was May Wilson. She bent down beside Steele and took hold of the bloody towel and applied pressure.

Steele rose to his feet and took his gun out of his ankle holster. All eyes grew wide at the sight of the gun.

Miss Wilson looked at Steele with a questioning stare. "Mr. Reid, why do you have a gun?"

"I'm not Mr. Reid. I'm actually a private investigator. My name is Richard Steele." He scanned the group. "There still may be a perpetrator on the premises. Everyone stay in this room as I go look around the house and the grounds."

Poppy got off the phone. "I talked to the police. They are on their way along with an ambulance." She looked at Steele who was moving towards the door. "Sergeant McMurphy told me to tell you he is on his way. He said to meet him at the entrance to the house to fill him in on what is going on."

Steele kept his focus on her. "Poppy, are you willing to come with me as I search the premises? I need someone who knows the layout of this house."

Poppy looked to Eve for her approval, as Eve had gone to be by her husband's side.

"Yes," Eve said. "Mr. Steele is trustworthy. He's here because I hired him to conduct an investigation for me."

As Poppy walked with Steele towards the door, suddenly another man rushed into the room. Steele raised his gun, only to have it lowered by Poppy.

"He's safe; that's my husband, Ralph."

The man, who appeared to be slightly drunk by his flushed cheeks, looked to Mr. Hamilton laying on the floor.

"What happened? Is he shot?"

"Yes, he is," Eve replied. "Why are you here, Ralph? Checking up on your wife because you think she is having an affair with my husband?" Eve directed an accusatory finger. "Maybe you're the one who did this! You own a gun, and it's no secret you have made threats in the past because of your jealousy. It seems like quite a coincidence that you happen to show up here at the time he was shot."

"Look, I had nothing to do with this! Yes, I came here to confront my wife again, but that is all. I would not do something like this."

Steele scanned the group. "Listen, I don't want anyone to leave this room. As far as I'm concerned, you're all suspects."

One by one each person objected to Steele's suspicions in murmuring voices.

The sirens of the police cars and ambulance grew louder as they entered the grounds of the house.

May Wilson looked over at Steele. "So, your name is Mr. Steele and not Mr. Reid? After the time we spent together talking to one another, I thought you would be a better judge of character than to *accuse me* of being a suspect."

Steele saw the hurt in May's eyes. He knew her statement was more than just an accusation of one acquaintance to another. At that moment he knew she felt something for him, the way he was starting to feel *for her*. But Steele had a job to do. He couldn't let his personal feelings get in the way of this investigation which had taken another turn. He needed to be objective.

He held her gaze. "I'm sorry May, but I have to be impartial here. I have a job to do, and nobody in this room is above suspicion." He looked at Poppy. "Since the police are already here, I'll have them search the whole house and the grounds. In the meantime, can you gather any items, such as purses brought here by anyone in this room? Then bring them back here as I want to go through them one by one for any evidence."

Eve rose to her feet. "I'll do it, Mr. Steele. As you said, no one is above suspicion—even Poppy. Therefore, I think I should be the one who gathers those things for you."

"Are you sure, Eve?" he said and glanced at Mr. Hamilton.

"Yes, there is nothing I can do right now for Randall. I'll gather all the purses and belongings and bring them back here," she said and wiped a tear from her eye. "It's hard seeing him lying on the floor like this."

"Alright, go ahead, Eve." He turned to the group. "No one is to leave this room until I or Sergeant McMurphy says so."

As Eve began to leave to gather the belongings, Daniel Thomas raised his hand. "I'm sorry, but I need to use the restroom really bad! If I don't, it is going to get messy in here."

Poppy raised her hand. "I need to use the lady's room also. I'll go there and come right back."

Steele allowed them to go, as Daniel immediately rushed into the bathroom in the hallway. Poppy then had to go to the bathroom on the other side of the house, in the hallway where the entertainment room was located.

Steele left the group, then met Sergeant McMurphy and his men as they were coming in the front door.

He greeted with a firm handshake. "I'm glad you're here, Sergeant. Have the ambulance medics go down the hallway on the right, then make a left and over to the last door on the left. The owner, Mr. Randall Hamilton has been shot. He is bleeding pretty badly and is currently unconscious. If you could, have your officers secure the house and grounds for the perpetrator. I'll fill you in on the rest after you instruct your officers."

After Sergeant McMurphy was finished instructing his men, Steele told him why he was there at the house in the first place. How he was hired by Eve Hamilton to gather evidence of a possible affair on the part of Mr. Hamilton. He told him the basics of why he suspected Miss Wilson and Miss Thomas because of the conversation they overheard about purchasing a gun. Also, that the brother, Daniel, might also have a motive because of the resentment he has towards Mr. Hamilton. He also let him know that Mr. Ralph Sorenson might have a motive also. He has threatened Mr. Hamilton before and accused him of having an affair with his wife. It is also known that he owns a gun.

After the house and grounds were searched where no one was found, Steele and Sergeant McMurphy went back into the study where the group of people was waiting.

The medical personnel had performed their emergency treatment on Mr. Hamilton and were just about ready to cart him off on a stretcher.

Eve walked over to Steele. "All of the purses and gift boxes brought here because of his birthday, are sitting over there on top of the wet bar; except for mine which I have with me. You are welcome to search mine if you like."

Steele had Eve open her purse. "Sorry, but just covering all the bases."

"No problem, I understand."

He moved a few items around. "Looks all clear; only normal things like makeup items, your car keys, and some driving gloves."

Eve closed her purse. "If there isn't anything else, I'm going to follow the ambulance to the hospital. When you're all done here, take a cab to Brookside Hospital and I can let you know his condition. Then we can drive back to the hotel."

Steele placed a sympathetic hand on her shoulder. "Are you going to be alright?"

Eve glanced at her husband being carted off on a stretcher. "I don't know. It's funny how some of the trivial things in life fade away when a person's life is on the line. It makes you think."

After Eve had left the room, Steele turned to Sergeant McMurphy. "Do you want to conduct these interviews or should I?"

"I think since you are fully aware of what is going on here, you should go ahead and start with your questioning. I'll be here to ensure that proper procedures are followed."

Steele gathered the groups' attention. "Okay everyone, I am sorry you have had to wait. However, since we could not find the perpetrator in the house or on the grounds, we can assume that person has already fled the scene. Or the alternative is that *one of you* had attempted to murder Mr. Hamilton."

"This is a total outrage!" said Daniel. "How can you sit here and accuse us of trying to kill someone? What grounds do you have to make assumptions like that?"

Steele held up his hands in halting fashion. "Listen, Sergeant McMurphy and I are just here to try to get to the truth."

"The truth?" May interjected. "If you want the truth, why don't you start with the truth of who you *really are*? When you came into our office you said your name was Jeffrey Reid. Now you tell us your name is Richard Steele."

"May, I'm sorry for hiding the truth of who I was. But I needed to take on the persona as a regular citizen and not a private eye."

"But why were you investigating Mr. Hamilton in the first place? Did you suspect that someone was going to attempt to kill him?"

The rest of the group chimed in their agreement with May's assertion.

Steele held up his hands once more. "Wait, please calm down everyone. I'll tell you the complete story."

Ralph Sorensen began to walk towards the door. "I'm not staying around here for no story; Poppy and I are going home!" He took Poppy by the arm and began leading her to the door.

Steele motioned Sergeant McMurphy to stop them. "Not so fast, you two. You can all leave when we are done asking you some questions." He raised his voice. "Ladies and gentlemen, this is a crime scene. And according to Mr. Steele, he has reason to believe you need to be questioned, so I am going to afford him some time to do just that."

Ralph Sorensen made a disgusted face but filtered back into the room with Poppy by his side.

Sergeant McMurphy motioned to Steele that he had the floor.

"Okay everyone, let me start at the beginning. I, as a private investigator, was approached by Mrs. Eve Hamilton to conduct an investigation into her husband. She suspected that he was having an affair. The three women in question were, Miss May Wilson, Miss Darlene Thomas, and lastly Mrs. Poppy Sorensen. After my initial investigation, I did not think he was having an affair with either Miss Wilson or Miss Thomas. However, in the course of our investigation," Steele paused. "The reason I say *'our'* is I have a partner who helps me on these investigations. Anyway, as we were spying on Miss Thomas, we saw she had a meeting with Miss Wilson. In the course of that conversation, they mentioned the fact they were going in as partners to buy a gun."

Most in the group caught their breath at this revelation. Miss Thomas's brother, Daniel stepped forward.

"Stop, nobody say another word! I have dealt with the court system before and I know we have rights. Mr. Steele, we are evoking our right to have an attorney present the next time you wish to question us." He looked around the group. "Are we all in agreement on this?"

"Yes, they all said."

Sergeant McMurphy glanced at Steele with a telling look. "That's it, Mr. Steele, we have to honor that request; no more questioning."

Steele glanced towards the wet bar. "Can we at least look inside the purses and boxes of gifts to make sure somebody didn't hide the gun?"

Sergeant McMurphy nodded his head. "Yes, considering this is a crime scene, we have the right to check their possessions to search for weapons."

Ralph Sorenson spoke up. "If all it takes is looking into a few purses and gift boxes, then I'm all for it. We just want to get out of here."

One by one Steele and Sergeant McMurphy rummaged through the purses but found nothing of consequence. When it came to one of the gift boxes, May Wilson stepped forward.

"Listen, when you open that box with the blue ribbon, do not overreact. I'll tell you right now, there is a gun inside."

Once more a gasp went up amongst the group. Some began to look at Miss Wilson with suspicion.

Miss Thomas added. "It's not what you think, Mr. Steele."

He took the ribbon and the top off of the box and looked inside. However, based upon what he saw, a look of revelation rose upon his face.

He took hold of the gun and held it before the group. It was a French navy flintlock pistol circa 1715. One which would require black powder from a powder flask, and a round lead ball. It was obviously not the weapon used to shoot Mr. Hamilton.

Steele looked at May. "So this was a gift to add to Mr. Hamilton's collection for his birthday?"

"Yes, it was supposed to be a surprise. One, we were helping Poppy with setting up the main entertainment room with decorations for Mr. Hamilton's birthday. Secondly, Miss Thomas's brother, Daniel, came with us because he heard Mr. Hamilton wanted to talk with him. Mr. Hamilton told me he wanted to settle things with Daniel regarding their past dispute. Daniel figured it would be better today without all the other guests around. He was waiting to talk with him as he knows Mr. Hamilton works in his office until 6:00 pm."

Steele glanced at the three of them. "And that's why all of you are here today?"

"Yes, that's correct; not to attempt to kill him. I don't know how you could have thought such a thing." May directed to Steele a look of disappointment, then turned her eyes away.

Then little by little all eyes began to drift towards Ralph Sorensen.

He took notice. "Hey, wait for just a second! Just because this particular gun was a gift, that doesn't mean that I'm the only suspect here. The brother there, Daniel, has a motive because of what Mr. Hamilton did to him with that real estate deal—Poppy told me all about that. Besides, this gun given as a gift could be just a front. Maybe they bought that vintage gun as part of their alibi as to why they are all here today. Also, to deflect the blame to someone else, like me."

Daniel stepped forward. "Hey, don't blame us for this. My sister and May had nothing to do with trying to kill him. Plus, me coming out here was a last-minute decision. I didn't intend to come, but my sister thought it would be good for me to try to work it out with Randall. She even suggested that I be the one to give Randall the gift as a gesture that I wanted to let bygones be bygones."

Ralph stood with his hands on his hips. "Well don't start pointing fingers at me and Poppy either. Did I have problems with him spending so much time with my wife—yes. And did I verbally threaten him that there would be trouble if he ever touched her—yes. But most of the time when that happened, I was drunk. I would start to drink and I would let things build up in my head. Then the next thing I knew, I was over here yelling at both my wife and Mr. Hamilton. But I'll tell you this, I did not try to kill him. And just to prove that I'm being upfront about all of this, the gun I own is in the glove compartment of my truck. If one of the police officers wants to go out with me to the car, I can show it to them. Now, I did use my gun about a week ago so the barrel will smell recently fired. We live out in the country, and we have this darn raccoon that gets into our trash all the time, so I used it on the rascal."

Sergeant McMurphy motioned for one of the officers to go with him to his truck. He also instructed the officer to search the other vehicles as well.

Poppy turned to Steele. "He's telling the truth. He did shoot that raccoon."

A host of eyes laid upon Poppy, as there was a trail of uncertainty in her voice.

Steele interjected. "Okay, let's not jump to any conclusions. There still needs to be a lot of investigating that we need to do."

They waited about ten minutes, then the group heard footsteps coming down the hallway. The officer and Ralph Sorenson came through the door. The officer, opened a handkerchief as to not place any new prints on the gun and held it before Sergeant McMurphy.

"Sir, as you can see, I found a .38 in the glove compartment. And yes, it was recently fired. I also searched the other vehicles on the grounds, but did not find anything."

Sergeant McMurphy took hold of the gun with the handkerchief and smelled the barrel.

"This barrel has the smell of a gun which was just recently fired; not a week ago. And considering that Mr. Sorenson has a motive of threatening Mr. Hamilton, which he admitted himself, I can only conclude that Ralph Sorenson may have committed this crime." He motioned to one of his officers. "Cuff Mr. Sorenson and place him under arrest! Mr. Sorenson, you are under arrest for the attempted murder of Mr. Randall Hamilton. You have the right to remain silent, anything..."

"No!" shouted Poppy. "I swear to you; he only shot that raccoon!"

Sergeant McMurphy finished with reading his rights.

Ralph turned to Poppy. "Baby, I didn't do it. But since I'm in cuffs, I might as well admit to the whole truth. The reason why that gun smells so recently fired; is I shot it just this morning. Them dang kids were kicking our trash cans at the edge of the road again on their way to school. I went to my truck and pulled out the gun, then I yelled at them and fired in the air to scare them. But that's all I did; I didn't shoot nobody."

As the officer carted off Ralph Sorenson, Poppy placed her hands to her face and began to weep.

May walked over and placed a consoling hand on her shoulder. "It will be alright. All we have to do is run through the events that happened, and then we can prove where your husband was at the time of the shooting."

Steele's eyes grew wide. "That's it! May, that's a great idea! What we need is for everyone to come back out here next weekend starting at six o'clock. We can reenact exactly where all of us were at the time of the shooting. I think it will reveal who we can rule out as suspects and who this crime points to."

"And if we don't want to come back out here to reenact the crime?" said Daniel in a combative tone.

Steele directed to him a stern look. "Then we will just have to subpoena you." He looked at Sergeant McMurphy. "Right, Sergeant?"

"That's exactly, right." He looked around the room. "And that goes for all of you. We will meet back here a week from today." He looked towards Steele. "Who has the keys to open the house for us to get in?"

"Mrs. Hamilton has the keys, and other than Mr. Hamilton, Poppy has all the keys to the house."

Sergeant McMurphy turned to Poppy. "I'm sorry, but I can't have you coming into the house unescorted. This is still a crime scene and my officers will be going over it with a fine-tooth comb." He reached out his hand. "Please give me the keys to this house. If your husband is proven innocent, then you will get them back." He scanned the group. "Again, is everyone in agreement to be back here a week from today?"

They all nodded their heads in agreement.

As May was getting ready to leave out the door, Steele quickly walked over and tapped her shoulder.

"May, I'm so sorry. I was just doing my job."

She directed a piercing stare. "Your job? So, let me get this straight. Your job is to impersonate someone you are not. Then lie to both me and Mr. Hamilton on the reason you were in our office. Act like you are making general conversation with me, yet all the time trying to gather information for your investigation. Then come back a second time to get more information—like the date for Mr. Hamilton's party. And in the course of all that, you use your smooth talk and charming ways to get me to let my guard down to solicit more information from me. If this is what you do in the 'course of your job,' then you are not the kind of man I thought you were. Mr. Steele, we will have to see each other next week to conduct this reenactment, but after that, please do not come around the office again. If I never see your face again, it will be too soon."

May turned and walked out of the room. Steele felt an ache lay on his heart as if he just lost something. He hadn't felt anything close to that since his wife had passed away.

Sergeant McMurphy walked up to Steele. "Tomorrow during the day, my men are going to conduct a thorough search of the house for any further clues. I have to get back to the station, but if you need a ride, I can drop you off at the hospital."

"Yes, I would be much obliged if you could do that. I do have a question... will I be able to get into this house to conduct my own investigation?"

He glanced to the side. "You said Mrs. Hamilton has keys to this house?"

"Yes, she does."

"I don't want her to come into this house until my men are completed with their search. Can you notify her of this for me? Then after my men are done, I can have one of my officers let you in with the keys we got from Mrs. Sorenson."

"Sounds good, thank you."

Sergeant McMurphy looked around the room. "Tell me, Mr. Steele, do you think we have our killer in custody?"

He teetered his head back and forth. "Honestly, I don't know what to think. So far, the prevailing evidence does point to Ralph Sorenson. But I will tell you this; the way this case has gone, I think this is only the beginning of figuring out this whole thing."

Chapter Ten

After Steele met Eve Hamilton at the hospital, the two went back to the hotel. Eve advised him that her husband had surgery to remove the bullet and he was still unconscious. The doctors were worried that perhaps his brain went without air for a short period, due to a blood clot. They said if he didn't wake up within the next few days, he could permanently remain in a comatose state, and eventually die.

The next morning on the drive back to Charlotte, Steele attempted to console Eve. She didn't say very much on the way back, only that she felt like a hypocrite in shedding tears for Randall when she wanted to divorce him.

After she dropped him off, Steele headed up the steps to his office where Kit was holding down the fort. After a brief conversation of the going's on, Steele began to tell Kit every detail as to what happened with Mr. Hamilton being shot. Kit sat in amazement as the story unfolded. After he was done, she shook her head at all that had transpired.

"And how is Mr. Hamilton? Is he going to be alright?"

A look of uncertainty rose upon his face. "Honestly, I don't know. He was in pretty bad shape when they took him to the hospital."

"But you said he talked to you before he passed out?"

"I wouldn't call it talking. He looked up at me and said the word, 'chair.' I asked him, what about the chair? In a weakened voice, he said, 'chair, moved.' Then he passed out."

"What do you think that means?"

"I have no idea. But I do know one thing, it must have been important. When someone thinks they are dying, they don't say things that don't matter, and they always say the truth. Those words must have great significance for him to say them at what he thought was his dying breath."

"So, what's next? You mentioned you are to go back to Southport to reenact the crime scene?"

"Yes, but since we have all week, I want us to use this time and start back at the beginning of our investigation. Specifically, the parts which led us to talk to Greenie and the people who came to him asking for information. For example, that man who approached him on where to buy certain types of guns. And the woman who wanted information about ammo for a .38., where that same woman wanted information on where to find a safe-cracker and or a locksmith. If we can figure some of that out, I think it will lay out the foundation for our possible suspects. This can then be used to fill in the blanks when we conduct the reenactment."

"But what about Ralph Sorenson? You don't think they have the right man in custody?"

"It very well could be him. He had a motive and the right caliber gun. However, it's strange to think that if he had shot Mr. Hamilton, he would have placed the weapon back in his glove compartment."

Kit interjected. "Or maybe that was a sly move. Didn't you say he told the police the reason the gun was recently fired is that he shot in the air as a warning to those kids? What I mean, is if he wanted that to be his cover story, then it makes sense he would have placed the gun right back in his glove compartment. If he tries to hide it somewhere else and they find it, then that would make him guilty of trying to hide the evidence. This way it goes along with his story; don't you think?"

Steele gazed upon Kit in admiration. "You are getting so good at this. And yes, if Mr. Sorenson had thought it through, you're right, then he would have placed it back where he last used it. However, he doesn't appear to be the sharpest tool in the shed—if you know what I mean. And secondly, he was on his way to getting drunk, so I don't know if he had the wherewithal to keep to his plan. But you do bring up a good point. Before the actual re-enactment, we will do a trial run. I want to see if Ralph Sorenson had time to shoot Mr. Hamilton, then go into the bedroom, then out a window, then over to his truck and place the gun inside."

"Do we know what type of bullet it was that shot Mr. Hamilton to match the gun of Mr. Sorenson?"

"Oh, that's right, I forgot to tell you about that. When I was in the hospital the doctor said the bullet they pulled out of him was a .38. But here's where I have a problem with Ralph Sorenson being the only suspect. There was also a woman who approached Greenie asking about bullets for a .38. And besides, why would Ralph Sorenson drive three hours to Charlotte to buy bullets for his gun, when he and Poppy live on the outskirts of Southport—it makes no sense. And even though right now it points to him having just fired his gun, I want to be thorough. As the saying goes, I don't want to leave one stone left unturned. And even though it's hard to believe that May Wilson had anything to do with this, I'm not ready to give up the thought that Darlene's brother, Daniel, could be still a suspect. When May and Darlene first walked into the study after Mr. Hamilton was shot, the brother didn't come into the room until a little bit later. So, where was he that he didn't come along with the two women? Was he hiding the gun? Also, he could have used the circumstances to his advantage when Darlene asked him to find a guy who sold vintage guns. Yes, they did buy the flintlock pistol as a gift, but that doesn't mean Daniel didn't buy another gun someplace else. He has just as much of a motive as Ralph Sorenson; maybe more. Ralph's issue was simple jealousy, but Mr. Hamilton ruined Daniel's life where he lost everything."

Kit rose to her feet. "Do you want me to get the file so we can go through our notes?"

"Yes, let's go through it with a fine-tooth comb. Maybe there is something in there that will make sense now that we know of the attempt on Mr. Hamilton's life."

Kit brought the file over to his desk. Steele opened the folder and began to read the notes they had on the case so far.

"Okay, I'm reading the part where it says the two women are talking at the country club. May gives Darlene the envelope full of money, then Darlene mentions she talked to her brother about getting the gun. Then Daniel makes the statement to make sure it is plenty loaded. On one hand, he could have been joking, but on the other hand, it could show intent on his part."

"Yes, that's true."

Steele read further. "Then the next part says Daniel wants to be the one to go to The Alley to talk to the man who was in the military—which we know was Greenie. This opens the possibility that Daniel may have thought this was the perfect opportunity for him to get even with Mr. Hamilton. In turn, when he went to the gun shop, he might have purchased another gun. At this point May and Darlene might not have not been involved in what Daniel was thinking. Daniel might have thought to kill Mr. Hamilton all on his own. Then my notes say that Greenie told me the man he spoke to had brown hair and a mustache. Well, guess what? Daniel has brown hair and a mustache, so that adds to the fact that it was likely Daniel who approached Greenie. Daniel also had the perfect cover story for being there at Southport. He could say that May and Darlene told him that Mr. Hamilton wanted to speak to him that weekend."

Kit took hold of the sheet of notes. "However, right here May says, 'I'm the one who has had lessons at a shooting range, so I know how to handle a gun. Even just holding one can make a person shaky.'" Kit directed to Steele a pondering stare. "Rick, you say you want to make sure not to leave a stone left unturned.

But isn't the fact that you are sweet on Miss Wilson blocking you from lifting the stone underneath her? Every step of the way, you keep making arguments for her not being involved in this."

Steele lowered his gaze for a moment, then back to Kit. "I'm not admitting anything about being sweet on her. But yes, you are right, I shouldn't discount her. However, that particular gun they were talking about, could not have been the weapon used to shoot him. Remember the bullet found inside Mr. Hamilton was .38, not from a vintage flintlock."

"Yes, but once again, that doesn't mean they didn't buy another gun—the one that shot Mr. Hamilton."

"That's true, and it certainly doesn't clear Daniel. What I need to do is go to the places where Greenie suggested Daniel find the gun. Maybe I can find out if there was a man who purchased a vintage flintlock, and also purchased a separate gun—a .38."

Steele rose to his feet. "Okay Kit, after I investigate the gun shops, we'll come back to our notes and try to fill in more of the blanks. Right now, I have a couple of gun shops I need to visit."

Steele decided to go to Mack's Guns on 4th Street first. After a brief conversation with the salesman, he knew this was not the place. The shop only sold modern guns, not vintage guns, and it was not a place that would have a back room. He then drove over to Hanover Guns & Pawn. As he walked in the door, the salesman was busy with another customer. However, looking into a particular display case, he knew he was in the right place. There were several vintage guns they had on display.

After a moment the salesman walked over to Steele. "Can I help you with something?"

Steele decided to play this on the up-and-up, just in case this man's testimony was needed at a hearing.

He pulled out his Private Investigator's license. "My name is Steele, Richard Steele."

The man looked over the ID. "I knew you were either a cop or some other type of flatfoot—you have that look."

Steele flipped the ID back in his pant pocket. "I need a little information about someone who might have come into this shop a few weeks ago looking to buy a vintage gun. Specifically, a vintage flintlock."

The salesman pointed to his pocket. "That ID of yours isn't going to buy you any information." The man glanced around the room. "Nothing in this shop is for free."

Steele knowingly nodded his head. "I get it," he said and dug into his other pocket. "How about now?" he said and handed the man a quarter.

The man looked at the single coin. "A quarter?"

Steele countered. "Hey, I only make a buck-seventy-five per hour. I figure it should be worth a few minutes of your time."

"If that's how much you make, then you're in the wrong line of work, buddy."

Steele huffed a sigh then pulled out another quarter and handed it to him.

"Fine," the man said, then he looked around to make sure no one was listening.

"There was a guy in here about a week ago looking to buy a vintage gun as you say."

"Do you remember what he looked like?"

"If I recall, he had brownish hair, and I believe a mustache."

Steele caught the description and held an inner smile. "Did he buy the gun?"

"Yeah, and he must have had deep pockets. I say that because the gun he wanted to buy was a first-run model which is very rare. Harry, the man who owns this shop, went back and forth with the guy for a while on the price. The man bargained pretty good, but still, he paid quite a bit for that gun."

"Can you tell me anything else? Like if that was the only gun he bought?"

"That I cannot tell you at any price."

"Why do you say that?"

"Because after the purchase of the vintage gun, the guy leaned in and asked Harry a question which I couldn't hear. Harry then took him into the backroom, which let's just say, has a variety of street items. Anyway, they were in there for a while, and when the guy came back out he seemed satisfied by the look on his face."

"So, did he buy another gun?"

"As I said before, I can't tell you that."

"Why?"

"Because what goes on in that back room with Harry, stays in that back room. Anything that goes on in there, people take to their graves."

Steele nodded his head. "I get it." He glanced at the man's nametag and extended his hand. "Thanks for the information, Nick, you've been a great help. I definitely got my fifty cents worth."

As Steele was about to leave out the door, the man called out to him. "Hey, Steele, here's a freebie. That guy you're asking about, not only did he leave with a contented smile, but he left with something very heavy in his front pocket."

Steele nodded his head. "Thanks, and I know I didn't hear that from you."

***

Steele returned to the office where Kit had just finished with her lunch. She tossed the empty sack in the trash.

"So, did you find anything out?"

"I think we might have another suspect."

"Really?"

"Yes, not only did the salesman identify the man as having brown hair and a mustache like Daniel, but I believe he bought another gun from the back room."

"Why do you say, *you believe* he bought another gun? And what is the back room?"

"A back room is a place where things are bought and sold under the table. They might be stolen items or things bought from street dealers and the like. With guns, it could be one found discarded in a back alley, or has had the serial number filed off so it can't be traced."

"But why did you say *you think* the brother Daniel bought another gun; don't you know?"

"No, because when things are bought from the back room, it is never spoken of. The only thing the salesman could tell me was that the man left with something very heavy in his front pocket."

"A gun?"

"I can't be sure, but the pieces are starting to fall in place. Once again, when we go through the reenactment, I will be looking to see if things match up with Daniel being a possible suspect."

"Should we go through what else we have as far as notes?"

"Yes, read what we have next."

Kit opened the folder and lifted the paper to eye level. "The next note in the file is on the mystery woman. The one who asked Greenie about a safecracker, a locksmith, and also about bullets for a .38."

"Yes, this mystery woman intrigues me. By his description of her being a good-looking woman behind her bandana and sunglasses; my first thought was May Wilson. However, it also could have been Eve Hamilton. Now if Eve was the one who approached Greenie, it could be for two reasons. One, she like May and Darlene, wanted to get her husband a gift for his birthday. Perhaps the bullets were to go along with a gun she already bought him for his collection. Or the other reason, which is hard for me to believe, would be that she wanted bullets because she herself wanted to kill him. The problem with that theory, is why would she want to kill him now that she is gathering evidence to divorce him? She told me the Will says she will only get half of what Mr. Hamilton's firm has made since they got married. The rest of the money would go to another party, perhaps a relative or some to the law firm. If she were to kill him, she would not get nearly as much as she would get in a divorce court."

"Yes, it wouldn't make sense for her to try to kill him."

"Now this mystery woman also asked if all .38 bullets were the same and would work on a turn of the century model. So, if this mystery woman *was* Eve Hamilton, she probably bought him a collectible gun as a gift, and she wanted the bullets to go along with it. However, if it *was* Eve Hamilton, then why would she go to Greenie? Knowing her, she would have gone to a high-end gun shop, and not a street person like Greenie who lives at The Alley."

"That's true, but remember; she told me that she's on a budget and that her husband only gives her an allowance of spending. Plus, she wouldn't be able to ask her husband for more money, seeing how the gift was for him. Not to mention she is spending money to hire you for this investigation. So maybe things are a little tighter right now, and she needs to be frugal in buying him that gift."

Steele smiled. "Very good, Miss Kit. I think I might have to change the name on our sign to, Kittridge Lawson—Private Eye."

Kit smiled from ear to ear, as her dimples became more pronounced. "That does have a nice ring to it, doesn't it?"

She read more of the notes. "It also says this woman asked about a safecracker or a locksmith. It says that Greenie told her to go to either Henry's Locks on Grand or to see a guy named Denny at Murphy's Bar on the west side of town."

Steele glanced at the clock. "I have that interview with a potential new client in a half hour. By the time I'm done, it will be too late to try these locksmiths. Tomorrow I'll try to see what I can find out at the locksmiths, or this guy Denny at Murphy's Bar." He stopped and lowered his gaze as a pensive look drew upon his face.

Kit took notice. "What's the matter?"

"It's the thought of stepping foot into a bar. I haven't been in one in more than two years since I stopped drinking. I hate the thought of even going into a place like that—too many bad memories."

She laid a caring hand on his shoulder. "That part of your life is over. You're a new man now, and I'm so proud of the man you have become."

Steele turned and pulled Kit into a warm hug. "Thank you. And I have you to thank for helping me get on my feet. You have no idea what your friendship means to me."

Kit's eyes began to pool. "Alright, alright," she said and turned away to wipe a tear from her eye. "Enough of this mushy stuff. Time to get back to work."

Steele smiled. "Still the same Kit, I see."

"Would you want me any other way?"

"No, I like you just the way you are."

*****

The following morning, Steele got in his 39' Chevy Fleetline and headed downtown. He thought he would stop by Henry's Locks on Grand Avenue first. As he walked in through the front door, the ring of a bell alerted a man who happened to be making keys. He turned off the grinder, removed his gloves, and walked over to the counter.

"May I help you, sir?"

"Yes, if you don't mind, I'd like a little information?"

"You need directions or something?"

"No, not that kind of information. Information about a person who might have come in here more recently."

"Well, if you're not needing my services, I need to continue working." He pointed to a sign on the wall which read; Time is Money.

As the man went back to working the key by rubbing excess metal shavings with a steel brush, Steele reached for his wallet and extended a dollar.

"For your time," said Steele.

The man waved him off. "No, just ask your question."

"I want to know if a woman came in here looking to have a key made, or perhaps she needed a safe to be opened?"

The man glanced to the side. "There was a lady who came in here more recently. What did she look like?"

"This one you probably would have taken notice of. She was either dressed in an overcoat, a bandana and round sunglasses; or she was a pretty blonde with hair resting on her shoulders, dressed to the nines, and displayed a high society attitude."

A look of recollection grew on his face. "Oh yeah, that one. Unfortunately, I would have liked to see your second description of her, but she was dressed in that overcoat, bandana, and glasses. She came in here about two weeks ago, and said she wanted a duplicate key made."

"And do you remember what kind of key that was?"

"Yeah, I remember it, because it was for a Corbin Mortise lock."

"What's so special about that?"

"Well back in the late 1800s these locks became popular because they are very secure. If you used this type of lock, it's because you wanted extra security, or were guarding something valuable behind that door."

"I see. Did the lady say anything else?"

"No, she stayed quiet while I made the key. I charged her twenty-five cents, but I remember she gave me a dollar and told me to keep the change."

"Anything else you can remember?"

"No, but if you're looking for that dame for personal reasons, I would be careful with that one."

"Why do you say that?"

"There was just something about her. I can't quite place my finger on it, but she appeared like a nice lady on the outside, but it's like you could never completely trust her. Do you know what I mean?"

He nodded his head. "Yeah, I know exactly what you mean."

Steele offered some money again for his time, but the man refused. He added. "Just remember my shop if you ever need a locksmith."

Steele got in his car and jotted down a few notes as to their conversation. He started his car and headed to Murphy's Bar on the westside. As he slowly drove down the streets of this dreary commercial neighborhood, he recalled the first time he ever stepped foot in any bar. The bar was called Tony's. It was a classy joint with live upbeat music. He was new to the police force and dropped into the bar at the suggestion of some fellow officers. That's when he first got the taste for the booze, which destroyed part of his life.

He shook off those thoughts as he pulled his car to the curb. Only a few cars were parked in front of the joint—too early for the heavy drinkers. He exited his car and made sure to lock his doors. This was not the neighborhood to be trusting.

He took hold of the door which read "NOTICE – No persons under 21 allowed" and opened it. Steele walked in and was greeted by the smell of booze, cigarettes, and loneliness. He looked around the room which was darkened with soft lighting and approached the barkeep.

"What'll you have," the barkeep asked.

"I'm actually looking for someone; they call him Denny."

The barkeep looked Steele up and down, then motioned with the tilt of his head towards a man sitting in the back near the jukebox. The man was in a corner booth sitting by himself with a glass of whisky and a billowing cigarette in his hand.

Steele slowly walked over and stood before him. "Are you the one they call Denny?"

The man casually looked up, when his eyes grew wide with recollection.

"No, this can't be; Richard Steele?"

Steele narrowed his eyes as he tried to recognize the man's face. The man then took off his hat, when Steele's memories rushed into this mind.

"Sammy? Sammy the slug? What's with the new name of Denny?"

"You should know, Steele. When a man gets a certain reputation, he has to reinvent himself; I started with a new name." He looked Steele over. "And talk about reinventing, you have certainly cleaned up. Last time I heard, you had fallen to rock bottom and were slumming it with the bums at Skid Row, or whatever they call it here in Charlotte."

"They call it The Alley. And they're not all bums; some are good men who happened to fall on hard times. And some are veterans who have had trouble adjusting to civilian life after the war."

Denny took a drink then set it down. "So, what brings you here into this neck of the woods?"

"I'm now a private investigator, and I'm looking for information on a woman who might have approached you for a job."

Denny sat up abruptly and directed to Steele a piercing stare. "You dare come to me asking for my help after you sent me up the river for two long years on a B&E? You've got some nerve!"

"If I knew it was going to be you, Sammy, I would have never come to ask you for information. But since I'm here, how about it?" He reached for his wallet. "I can make it worth your time."

"Worth my time? You don't have enough money to make up for the two years I spent in that hell hole!" Denny took a puff of a cigarette and scanned Steele's attire. "Well look at you, the high and mighty have returned. What are you doing as a PI; sticking your nose where it doesn't belong like when you were on the force?"

Steele sharpened his focus. "What are you talking about? What do you know about my dealings when I was on the force?"

"Look, I heard things on the streets through the grapevine. I know you were promoted to investigator just after you busted me. I also know you started looking into underground businesses, that let's just say, had close ties to some of the boys in blue. And when you got too close, I heard they stole something or *someone* close to you."

Steele's eyes intensified. "What do you know about my wife's abduction?"

"Again, it was just rumors I heard while I was in the pen." Denny puffed another toke of his cigarette. "Oh, and it's a shame it ended badly. Honestly, I didn't think it would end that way. I heard the body was so badly burned, you couldn't even recognize her."

Steele's eyes blazed with fury. He reached over the table and yanked Denny by the shirt.

He cocked his fist. "Why you no good..." Steele's fist was trembling. It took all that was within him not to lay Denny out. He lowered his fist and shoved Denny back down in the booth.

"You're not worth it! You are, and will always be, Sammy the slug! A slimy character who leaves a trail of slime wherever you go!"

Denny adjusted his mangled shirt. "You're lucky you didn't touch me, Steele. I would have filed a police report for assault! And even though I don't have a good reputation, the local police force hates you more than they hate me."

Steele slammed his fist on the table. "The woman, Sammy! Did an attractive well-dressed woman approach you for a job? I need to know!"

Denny laughed. "Wow, either this case or this woman has got you by the cojones if you're sucking up to me for information."

"I know she approached you about doing an inside job. Come on, Sammy, tell me the truth for once in your life! She wanted you to get into a safe in an office building on Main Street, am I right?"

Denny leaned back with his arms resting on top of the booth. "Not on your life, Steele. The fact that you want this information so bad, makes it so much easier not to tell you. Besides, if this was an inside or illegal job, then why would I incriminate myself?"

Steele took a breath to calm himself. "Alright, I get it; but I'm no longer a cop."

He reached into his wallet and threw a five on the table. "Just something, Sammy; anything to let me know you at least spoke to her. You don't have to tell me if you took the job or not."

Denny glanced to the side, then reached out and took the five-dollar bill and placed it in his shirt pocket.

"Okay, Steele, you want something? The next time you see this '*alleged woman*', tell her that Denny's says hi, and she knows where to find me." He added. "Man, I tell you; that woman had a pair of shapely stems that went on for days."

Steele nodded his head. "Okay, thanks for the information."

Denny's face flushed with anger. "Look, you have nothing to thank me for! I told you nothing! Now get out of here! I don't want to see your sorry butt around here again!"

Steele walked out of the bar and over to his car. As he sat thinking about their conversation, he was still shaking from anger. He had thought that the passing of time had softened the hurt in his heart of the loss of his wife. But after his encounter with Denny, he realized it burned just as strong as ever.

Chapter Eleven

Steele didn't quite get the answers he was looking for from Denny, but it was something. Denny revealed he had spoken to someone who he thought was Eve Hamilton. Denny's comment about the woman having long shapely legs would point to Eve rather than May. May had attractive legs also, but you would not describe them as being long, as May was shorter than Eve. Steele had a hunch. He figured the reason Eve wanted a safecracker was to open the safe at her husband's office and get a look at the revised Will. He knew that when someone is named as a beneficiary to a Will, that if there is a change or revision, that each beneficiary must be notified. In turn, he figured Eve wanted to see if her husband had taken her out of the Will entirely; and to see the effective date of such a change.

As Steele got on his way, a thought entered his mind. There would be one person who might know if Eve ever tried to access Mr. Hamilton's office while he was not there—May Wilson.

He quickly made a U-turn and headed downtown. Knowing that May was very upset with him, he figured he would have to apologize first before trying to extract information from her. He just hoped she would not throw him out of the office on sight.

Steele drove up to the five-story building and parked his car. With a quick look in the review mirror, he ran a hand through his hair to assure it was in place. He took the elevator to the fifth floor and walked over to the office. As he opened the door and walked in, Miss Wilson looked up from her desk to see who it was.

Upon recognizing his face, she waved him off. "No, Mr. Steele, I told you I don't ever want to see you in this office again!"

"May, please; I need to talk to you. And please call me Richard."

May stood to her feet and moved toward him. "Get out! You have no reason to be here! And don't call me May; I'm Miss Wilson *to you*! You betrayed my trust, so we are no longer cordial to be calling each other by our first names."

"May, I just need a few minutes of your time and then I won't bother you again."

"Mr. Hamilton is fighting for his life, and all you can think about is getting information for your precious case?" May crossed her arms. "I'm not saying another word!"

"Okay, fine, then I will do all the talking. I need to know if Eve Hamilton ever got a look at the revised Will? I know that you looked at it because my partner Kit overheard you tell Darlene you looked at the revised Will. She said you made the statement that the revisions surprised you. Can you tell me what those revision were?"

May held her defensive posture. "Why should I tell you anything?"

"Because it could have a bearing going forward when we do the reenactment. I just want to make sure I cover all my bases. I'm not sure how this would have a bearing on proving who might have attempted to kill Mr. Hamilton, but I also want to make sure we put the right person behind bars, don't you?"

May held silent for a few moments. "I'm sorry, but I don't feel Mr. Hamilton would want me to divulge anything further."

"I understand. But can you at least tell me this one thing? Did Eve Hamilton recently come here and was in Mr. Hamilton's office alone? Or if perhaps another man was with her when she was in his office?"

May huffed a conceding sigh. "Okay fine. Now that you mention it, just last week I got a call from the janitorial service. They said the regular janitor was ill and so he would not be able to clean the office that day. I told them, fine, that Mr. Hamilton was not in the office anyway, so it could wait until tomorrow. Around the time the janitor usually makes his rounds to the fifth floor, Mrs. Hamilton arrived. Along with her was a man in a janitor's uniform, along with a ballcap, which the other janitor service never wears. She told me the janitorial service had called the house to advise Mr. Hamilton regarding the regular janitor not being able to clean today. Mrs. Hamilton then said, she decided to hire another company to fill in for the day, as she knows how particular her husband is about everything being clean. At first, I thought it was a little odd for her to get involved in something like this, but being Mr. Hamilton's wife, I let her into his office. While the man was cleaning, Mrs. Hamilton sat near me and started to talk. This was very unusual because in the past, she hardly ever says anything to me. At a point, the janitor said he was going to close the door because the vacuum was very noisy. Mrs. Hamilton waved her hand as if to say, go ahead, and the man began to vacuum. Then I heard the vacuum stop and he opened the door and asked Mrs. Hamilton to check his work to see if it was satisfactory. While she was in there, the man came out and started to clean up my trash and dusted off the furniture in the lobby area. A few minutes later Mrs. Hamilton came back out and said everything was fine. She then closed the door to his office and they both left."

"How long would you say the door was closed when the janitor was vacuuming?"

"Maybe five minutes."

Long enough, Steele thought, *for Denny to open the safe for Mrs. Hamilton to take a look at the Will.*

"And would you be able to describe him?"

"He was wearing a khaki color uniform. He appeared to have dark brown hair, but most of it was covered by the ballcap. I didn't get a good look at him because his cap was very low into his face."

Steele held out his hand to shake, but May refused. He withdrew his hand. "Thank you, May, for the information you gave me; I appreciate it very much. As I told you at the house in Southport, this is my job. I have to gather information when I work on a case, and sometimes I have to say I'm someone else to keep my true identity concealed. It's just part of my job."

"Yes, I understand what you do for a living. However, because you used those skills on *me*, I can no longer trust you. And even more so, when you used your charms and flattering words on me, then it became personal. In other words, you were willing to sacrifice my personal feelings for the sake of gathering some information. And for this, I cannot forgive you."

Her words hit Steele like a punch in the stomach. However, a punch in the stomach would have hurt far less than what Steele felt in his heart.

"Again, May, I'm so sorry. I hope that one day you can find it in your heart to forgive me."

May stayed silent as she watched Steele walk out the door.

*****

On Friday morning Steele arrived bright and early. After settling in, Kit arrived and placed her jacket on the coat rack.

"Morning, Rick. Sorry I couldn't make it in the last few days, but the supermarket manager wanted me to fill in for a girl who was sick."

"That's okay, don't worry about it."

"So, how did things go on the day you went to see about the safecrackers?"

"Really interesting. In a nutshell, I believe Eve Hamilton was the one who went to see that man, Denny, a safecracker. I actually knew him from when I was on the force when his name was Sammy. Let's just say, we were on the opposite side of the tracks. To make a long story short, he didn't want to give me much information, but he did let on that a woman, who I think was Eve Hamilton, did come to see him. He wouldn't say if he did a job for her, but I believe he did. After I left there, I went to talk to May Wilson."

"How did that go considering how upset she was with you?"

"She still is. And at first, she didn't want to talk to me at all. However, after a little coaxing, she finally did. She admitted to me she looked at the revised Will, but she wouldn't tell me what those revisions were. But she did say that just last week Eve Hamilton came into the office. I believe Eve called the cleaning service office and canceled the regular janitor from coming. When she arrived at the office, she had with her a man dressed as a janitor, but I believe it was Denny. To make another long story short, Denny was alone in Mr. Hamilton's office for enough time to open the safe. Then Eve Hamilton went in there and she must have looked at the revised Will."

"And where do you think it fits into the attempt on Mr. Hamilton's life?"

Steele scratched his head. "I'm not sure. If I only knew what the revised Will says, then I could draw a conclusion. For now, I'll keep that in the back of my mind moving forward with the reenactment."

"And when will you be traveling out to Southport for the reenactment?"

"Not just me—we will be going."

Kit perked up. "Really? I'm going with you?"

"Yes, I already asked your foster parents for permission and they said you can go. I assured them I needed you for this part of my investigation."

"Thank you! I rarely get a chance to go on a trip like this. And I know I might not be 'needed for the investigation' as you told them, but whatever you need I'll be there to help."

"Kit, I wasn't saying I need you for your foster parents' sake; I really do need you. I don't think you realize how much of a help you are to me. You are my sounding board when I need to talk out a case. And you always come up with suggestions or ideas that in turn, prompt me to think in a direction I hadn't before. I need another set of eyes to see things which I may not catch because I'll be the center of all that will be going on."

Kit smiled. "Then good, I'll be your eyes and ears. So, how are you going to do this reenactment?"

"Just like it sounds. I'm going to have everyone placed in their positions at the time the lights went out and Mr. Hamilton was shot."

"Have you heard any more information on how he is doing?"

"Yes, I talked to Eve the other day as she has been traveling back and forth. She said the doctors say he is now stable, but they are fearful he may never come out of his comatose state. And even worse than that, even if he does come out, the doctor fears there may be permanent damage to his brain where he will never be able to function."

"Oh no, that's terrible. Next time I'm in church I'll say a prayer for him."

"I may not be attending church services, but doesn't the Bible say that God is everywhere and can hear our prayers no matter where you are?"

Kit looked at Steele with admiration. "Very good; and you are right; He does hear our prayers wherever we are. I'll say one tonight before I go to bed."

"Speaking of going to bed, this reenactment will be in the evening. And by the time we are all finished, it will be too late to travel back home. I told your foster parents you would have to stay overnight and sleep in a motel room. Make sure you pack a little bag with toiletries and something to wear to bed. The room has two full beds; one for each of us. I would have gotten you a separate room; you being a young lady and all, but you're not old enough to stay in a room alone; you have to be eighteen."

"That's okay, as long as you don't snore too loud," she jested. "So, tomorrow is the big day, huh? I hope we find the person who tried to kill Mr. Hamilton. It's not right for the guilty person to get away with this."

"No, it isn't right." Steele glanced at the clock. "Why don't you just work until noon and take the rest of the day off. Then you can go home and get your things together for our trip. I want to leave bright and early tomorrow, so we will leave at eight."

"Isn't it only around three and a half hours trip?"

"Yes, but we will have to stop for lunch and bathroom breaks. Also, once we get there, we need to check into the motel room. Then I have made arrangements to get into the house in Southport a little early. Sergeant McMurphy is going to be there to let me in as I want to go over the crime scene before everyone gets there."

"That's a good idea. I hope this reenactment reveals the true perpetrator."

"So do I, Kit."

*****

The day broke like every other day as Steele glanced out the window of his apartment. However, as the sun began to rise in the sky, *this day* felt different. This reenactment he was about to undertake felt ominous at best. Sergeant McMurphy and his deputies were at a dead end after investigating the crime scene. He had phoned Steele last evening that his men did not find any more clues regarding the case. In regards to outdoor footprints, there were too many people, including landscapers, to make heads or tails as to who was coming or going. In the span of a couple of hours, he was going to have to figure out who the culprit was. Lives were going to be held in the balance, and it all fell on his shoulders. Yes, Sergeant McMurphy would be there to assist, however, he did not know what Steele knew. How he has followed the lives of these players in this scenario since the night

Eve Hamilton stepped foot into his office. But instead of having the luxury of weeks to complete the investigation, he would have to do it within a couple of hours. And it all came down to this reenactment.

****

The conversation was sparse between him and Kit as they journeyed their way to Southport. Kit mainly looked at the scenery with some small talk in-between. But knowing Rick as she does, she also knew when to stay quiet and leave Steele to his thoughts.

They arrived at the motel and checked into the room. Kit had never stayed in a motel, so she found it interesting. For Steele, it was only a place to rest his body, as his thoughts ran a mile-a-minute on all the conversations, facts, and investigative notes they had taken over the past month.

After resting a bit, he and Kit drove out to the Hamilton house where Sergeant McMurphy met him at the front door.

He greeted with a firm handshake. "Mr. Steele, I have some news on those gentlemen you wanted me to track down. Or maybe I should say, no news."

"What do you mean by that?"

"Out of the three college buddies of Mr. Hamilton, so far no one has returned my calls. One of them is on an excursion out of the country in Canada. I called the hotel he is staying at and the manager told me he was not due to return until this afternoon. I left a message for him to call you once he got in; saying it was urgent. I also left a message with the other two for them to get in touch with us here at this number."

"Very good, thank you. I just hope they call us back."

Sergeant McMurphy glanced around. "I don't know what you got going, but I hope it works out. Right now, all we have is circumstantial evidence against Ralph Sorensen. Without having a witness to him shooting Mr. Hamilton, he could get off with a good lawyer. Speaking of which, any news on the condition of Mr. Hamilton?"

"Not much more. The doctors are just hoping he comes out of that comatose state he is in."

"I wish him well. Such a shame for something like this to happen to a young man like that."

"Yes, it is." Steele looked around the room. "So, can I have free reign over the house and grounds?"

"Yes, I have to get back to the station, but I'll be back for the reenactment. I will bring Ralph Sorenson with me at that time. In the meantime, I left two deputies to help you with whatever you need."

"Good, I will definitely use them."

As Sergeant McMurphy left, Steele motioned to Kit to join him, as she was admiring a beautiful baby grand piano.

She scampered over. "I was just looking at that piano. Boy, these people are rich."

"Yes, they are. So, are you ready? Because we only have about an hour and a half before everyone gets here."

"Yes, what do you need me to do?"

"First of all, we are going to verbally go through the reenactment ourselves. We will go through each scenario and talk it through as to who was where at what time. At times, I may have you walk through the house to a particular person's spot where they claim they were located. Also, as we are conducting these tests, if you can't hear me calling out at times, have one of the deputies be a go-between. When we're done with all that, I want us to look carefully for any possible locations where we believe Mr. Hamilton has a hidden room of some sort, with other valuables. I'm waiting on a call from the three men who were with Mr. Hamilton a few months ago. Eve claims they were talking about his gun collection when Mr. Hamilton locked the study door. She then overheard one of the men say something about 'an interesting secret.'

"Okay, what's first."

"Let's start at the east hallway where the study is located. In that hallway, there is also a bedroom and a bathroom. Ralph Sorenson claims he was in his truck at the time the lights went out. However, I have a hunch he might have been in the house at that time. I want to time how long it would have taken for him to shoot Mr. Hamilton, then rush out the bedroom window, then back to his truck and place the gun in the glove compartment. I say this because May and Darlene said that after the gunshot, they saw Ralph getting out of his truck when they passed by the formal living room. So, when I say go, then point your finger and shoot me, then rush into the bedroom, out the window, then over to the gate where he was parked. Wait three seconds, for the time it would have taken him to place the gun in the glove compartment. I will be watching and I'll check the time at that point. Since the bathroom is next to the bedroom, it would have taken about the same time frame, so I don't think we need to do it twice. I also want to walk through a scenario which involves Daniel Thomas and his location when the lights when out and the gunshot when off."

"Okay, it's a good thing I brought my tennis shoes."

Steele and Kit ran through the exercises on both possible suspects. When they were finished, they entered the study and began to look around for a side panel or anything which could be a door to a hidden room.

After checking every corner of the room and not finding anything, he turned to Kit. "We're pretty much out of time. Anyway, I better take a few minutes to think this out on how I'm going to proceed with this reenactment."

Kit patted his shoulder. "Don't worry, I have confidence in you. I know you'll figure it out and find the person who attempted to kill Mr. Hamilton."

"Don't know what I would do without you, Kit?"

She smiled. "You would probably have more money in your pockets by not paying me as your office assistant."

Steele smiled. "Well, if we can figure this whole thing out, I won't need any money because I'll feel like a million bucks!"

Kit nodded her head. "So, will I."

***

The other guests soon arrived. It was now nearing the top of the hour at six o'clock, and all the players were ready and accounted for. Ralph Sorensen was in handcuffs, as Sergeant McMurphy had brought him in his squad car.

They were all standing there in the study when Eve Hamilton huffed a breath of impatience.

"Mr. Steele, are we ready to start this? I have a dinner date planned with a friend." She paused. "Well, that's after I visit my husband at the hospital."

"Yes, Eve, we are ready to begin. If you look around, we have Sergeant McMurphy present, and two of his deputies. They will be placed strategically throughout the house to view everyone's location. Now, I want all of you to go to the exact spot where you were when the lights first went out. For example, Miss Wilson and Miss Thomas, if you were placing streamers on the windows, then go to that exact window and act like you are placing streamers."

Daniel Thomas raised his hand. "What happens if you were in the bathroom at that time? The truth is, I had eaten some bad fish and it hit me when I was here at this house. Needless to say, I was back and forth to the bathroom."

"If you were in the bathroom, then go into the bathroom. Listen, everyone," he said and raised his voice. "Just go to your spots until either myself, Kit, or one of the deputies instructs you to move to the next location. When it is time to start, I will blow my whistle once. When you hear the whistle, that will indicate the lights went off. Since you may not be able to hear it on the other side of the house, Kit also has a whistle and will relay it down the hallway. When you hear the whistle, start to do exactly what you did that night and at the same speed. Then when you hear the whistle blow twice, stop moving. If you deviate from what you did that night, you are likely to be found out because of the others who were also in the house. Am I clear on this?"

"Yes," they all said in unison.

"Okay, go to the place you were that evening. And remember, wait for the whistle to move, and stop when you hear the whistle blow twice."

Everyone took their place, including Steele who was just outside the French doors to the study. However, he left the doors open to ensure Kit could hear his whistle.

The anticipation began to build within each player. Then suddenly, a strange sound broke the silence—Daniel had tooted a fart.

Darlene called out, "Daniel! Was that you?"

"I'm sorry, but Mr. Steele said to do 'exactly' what we did that night. And because of the gas I had from the fish, I tooted then also."

Laughter broke out from some of the players.

Eve conveyed her displeasure. "My goodness, don't you people have any class? Mr. Steele put this together to try to catch the person who attempted to kill my husband. The least you could do is show some respect!"

With her stern chastising, the laughter quickly faded and the house fell silent.

Steele looked at his watch as it was near the top of the hour. Poppy to her credit, did exactly as she did before. She went to the file cabinet and acted as if she was putting some files away. Suddenly, the grandfather clock chimed loudly just as it did that evening. Steele had instructed one of the deputies to wait fifteen seconds after the chime, then turn off the power to the electric panel located in the back patio. After waiting fifteen seconds, the lights went out. Steele blew his whistle loudly and at the same time, Kit blew her whistle as loud as she could. Poppy moved towards the door and began to walk down the first hallway. First, she passed the bedroom, but when she got near the bathroom, she turned slightly as a memory caught her attention. She knew she needed to continue walking down the hallway as instructed, so she did.

In the meantime, Steele was counting down the time he estimated passed between the lights going out and the gunshot. A few moments later, he felt it was time, so he entered the French doors and blew his whistle twice, as did Kit. Steele then walked through the study and into the hallway and over to where the two hallways intersected.

He raised his voice. "Okay everyone, you should be in the location you were when the gunshot went off."

Poppy called out. "No, this isn't right. I was further along when the gunshot went off. I was passing through the kitchen and was about to turn down the west hallway when I heard the shot. I abruptly stopped and called out to Mr. Hamilton, but he didn't answer me. I turned to head back towards the study when I heard a noise from the hallway like a door closing. I went back through the kitchen and into the hallway and that's when I saw Eve Hamilton near the door to the back patio. I was surprised she was there at the house and asked her about the noise which sounded like a gunshot. She commented that it was probably one of her husbands' guns that went off by accident. She told me to check on him and she would try to get the lights back on."

Steele pondered for a moment as to why Eve had moved from under the stairwell.

He called out, "Eve! Where are you? According to Poppy, you were standing by the back patio door?"

She moved out from under the stairwell. "I'm sorry, she's right. I forgot I moved from under the stairwell once I saw the lights go off. I didn't want that to interfere with our plan to catch my husband and Poppy together. I wanted to turn the lights back on before she left the study."

Steele nodded his head. "Okay, that makes sense." He called out, "Okay everyone, stay where you are. I'm going to see exactly where each of you are at this moment."

Miss Wilson and Miss Thomas were the closest in the large entertainment room. He walked in and glanced around the room.

"You people were not kidding at how big this room is. I think it's bigger than my whole apartment."

He looked in the corner of the room to see May on top of a ladder with a streamer in her hand, and Darlene was holding the ladder.

May spoke up. "This is exactly where we were when the lights went out and the gunshot went off. We didn't move when the lights when off because we thought they might come right back on—that happens a lot. Also, I didn't want to make any sudden moves down the ladder and break my neck."

Darlene added. "I was just holding the ladder. However, at that time I thought I heard an exchange of some words."

Eve and Poppy walked into the room. "That was us," said Eve. "I was about to go out the back door to turn the lights back on when I heard the gunshot. Poppy then rounded the corner and I told her to check on Randall, that one of his guns probably went off by accident. I then went into the back patio to the electrical panel and turned the lights back on, then hurried over to the study."

Steele gathered May, Darlene, Eve, and Poppy together. "Okay, did anyone notice anything different this time around? For example, was Daniel always in the bathroom, or was he helping with the decorations?"

Darlene spoke up. "He was helping us with the decorations before the lights went out, but then he had to rush to the bathroom. I believe he was in there all the time the lights were out and throughout the gunshot. Then as May and I rushed towards the study, I heard a flush, and then a few moments later Daniel came out of the bathroom and followed us."

Steele called out. "Daniel! Come over to the entertainment room with all of us."

Daniel exited the bathroom and made his way into the room.

"Darlene says you were in the bathroom at the time the lights went out and when the gunshot was heard. Is this correct?"

"Yes, I was using the toilet at the time the lights went out. I couldn't see that well, but fortunately, there was still enough light coming in through the bathroom window for me to finish my business."

Steele turned to Poppy. "From the time you heard the gunshot and briefly spoke to Eve, how much time was it until you turned the corner to the last hallway? And when you count that in your head, count one/one-thousand, two/one-thousand, and so on."

Poppy gathered her thoughts. "It was probably twelve seconds or so. I stopped in the kitchen, then had that quick exchange with Mrs. Hamilton for about three seconds, then rushed through the kitchen and down the first hallway and turned the corner. I was practically running, so like I said, maybe twelve seconds to turn the corner to the second hallway."

"Did you see anyone in the hallway at that time?"

"No, I didn't see anyone."

Steele took hold of his stopwatch. "Daniel, I need for you to go into the study and stand at the doorway. When I say go, you act like you shot Mr. Hamilton, then rush over to the bathroom and close the door."

"So, I'm still a suspect?"

"I just need to cover all the bases, so please just bear with me."

Daniel begrudgingly walked over to the study and did as Steele had instructed. When the exercise was done, the stop-watch stopped at five seconds.

"Okay, everyone. Based upon this exercise, Daniel would have had plenty of time to shoot Mr. Hamilton, then rush back into the bathroom before Poppy would have turned the corner and seen him."

Daniel began to protest when Poppy raised her hand. "Actually, when we were going through the first part of this reenactment, I recalled a few things I had forgotten about. After I left the study and was walking down the hallway, I thought I heard a door close and a toilet flush, but I don't think it was the same door. Also, no offense to Daniel, but when I passed the bathroom, it smelled really bad like one of those open cesspools."

Daniel sheepishly shrugged his shoulders. "Look, I ate some bad fish. But if the shame of me having diarrhea at the time of Mr. Hamilton's shooting gets me off, then I will be glad to shoulder the embarrassment."

Steele turned to Poppy. "And you're sure about what you heard and smelled?"

She nodded her head. "Yes, I'm positive."

Steele drew a thought. "If Daniel was in the bathroom and Poppy heard a door close, then who was in the bedroom?"

Sergeant McMurphy and Ralph Sorenson were standing a short distance off when this conversation was going on. After Steele made that statement, everyone turned and looked at Ralph Sorenson.

Seeing a host of eyes staring at him, he objected. "Wait a cot-ton-picking minute! Just because my wife said she heard a door close, doesn't mean I was in the bedroom. And that flush she heard, maybe Daniel was flushing the gun down the toilet. Did anybody think of that?"

Steele thought about that for a moment. He turned to Sergeant McMurphy. "Could a .38 make it down the toilet?"

Sergeant McMurphy searched through his thoughts. "That all depends. A short barrel snub-nosed .38 might make it at the right angle, but not a Smith & Wesson long barrel. Based on the bullet fragment pulled from Mr. Hamilton, I really couldn't say which one it was."

"You see!" said Ralph. "That goes to prove he could have tossed a gun down the toilet."

Daniel raised his voice. "He's just trying to deflect the blame! And besides, I don't own a gun!"

Steele interjected. "Actually, Daniel, you could have bought a gun while you were also purchasing the French navy flintlock pistol as a gift. I went into Hanover Guns & Pawn, and I found out that you bought something from the back room. If anyone here doesn't know what a 'back room' is, it's a private room for valuable or questionable items."

"I did no such thing!" Daniel retorted. "And how would you know anyway? When I walked out of that shop, I only had *one* package in my hand."

Steele pointed to his pant pocket. "When you walked out of that shop, there was something heavy sagging in your front pocket. Like maybe another gun?"

Daniel turned to Darlene. "Sis, the day I bought the vintage gun at Hanover's, I came over your house. Tell Mr. Steele what I brought you."

Darlene turned to Steele. "When Daniel came over that day, he gave me a present. When I opened it, it was a silver jewelry case. It was quite heavy as it was made of pure Sterling silver."

Daniel interjected. "I bought that jewelry case at Hanover's as a gift for my sister because she has been such an encouragement to me after I lost everything. I wanted to buy her something really nice, but I knew I couldn't afford a new one from a department store. When I went to the gun shop, I asked Harry, the shop owner, if he had anything nice as a gift for my sister. He took me into the back room and that's when I saw that particular jewelry box and I bought it. And because transactions in that back room are confidential, I placed it in my pant pocket away from view."

The look on Steele's face indicated he believed what Daniel was saying. "Okay, I believe you about the jewelry case. But that still doesn't mean you didn't buy another gun from some other shop."

Daniel shook his head. "Look, I only bought that vintage gun and the jewelry case and that's it."

Steele turned his attention to May and Darlene. "Okay, let's go back into the entertainment room. I want to run through exactly what the two of you did once you heard the gunshot."

They walked back to the room, as May climbed up on the ladder with a streamer in her hand and Darlene was holding the ladder.

"Alright," he said. "When I say go, you do exactly what you did after the gunshot. And do everything at the same speed. Then when you get to the area just past the kitchen where you saw Ralph Sorenson, stop. I'll check my stopwatch for the time."

Steele said go and started his stopwatch.

May spoke up first. "Right now, we heard the shot and looked at each other. It was darker in the room from the lights being out, so I told Darlene we should go see what is happening. We thought we heard someone talking which must have been Poppy and Eve. As I was about to step off the ladder with Darlene guiding me down, the lights came back on. I turned and handed Darlene the streamer and then we heard someone rushing through the hallway, which we now know was Eve."

Steele clicked the stopwatch. "Okay, wait just a second." He turned to Eve. "When you rushed through the hallway by the open door to the entertainment room, did you see both May and Darlene in that room?"

"No, I didn't see either of them. When you pass by that room from the hallway, you only see the area of the room in front of the door. Plus, I was rushing to get to the study because of the gunshot."

May interjected. "Why are you asking Eve if we were in the room? Do you think we are lying about where we were at that time?"

"May, I am just getting statements to corroborate each of your stories."

May folded her arms. "Meaning, you don't believe us?"

"No, meaning, I have to cover all aspects of this investigation and then try to piece it all together. I have found that if you miss a piece, you might not be able to solve the puzzle."

Steele turned to Darlene. "Darlene, please continue from the point where May left off." Steele started his stopwatch again.

"Okay, after May climbed down from the ladder, then we placed the streamer paper on the table. We then walked to the door into the hallway. We then walked through the kitchen and entered the living room. This is when we looked out the front window and saw Ralph Sorenson closing the door to his truck."

"Stop!" said Steele. He looked at the stopwatch. "That took you twenty-six seconds to get down from the ladder, place things on the table, then walk out the door and down the hall, through the kitchen and into the living room, then look out the window." He turned to Kit. "How long did we time it for Ralph Sorenson to shoot Mr. Hamilton, then out the window, and then over to his truck?"

Kit looked at the notes. "It took twenty-four seconds."

All eyes slowly filtered over to Ralph Sorenson. Once again, he teetered his head back and forth.

"Oh no you don't! You're not going to pin this on me because of some test. I'm telling you the truth; I did not shoot him!"

Tears began to flow from Poppy's eyes. She walked over and stood before him.

"Ralph, look at me." He shook his head in the negative. "Yes, Ralph, as your wife I am asking you to look me in the eye." Ralph lifted his head and gazed into her tear-filled eyes. "Please, tell me the truth, did you do this?"

"No, I'm telling you the truth, I did not shoot Mr. Hamilton."

Poppy looked intently into his eyes. "I know you, Ralph, there is something else you are not saying. Tell me what that is."

"If I do, it will only go to prove to everyone that I did it."

"You don't know that. Maybe what you tell us will bring some other evidence as to who really did this."

Ralph looked into her eyes. "I'm so sorry, baby. But I wasn't telling the whole truth. The fact is, *I was* in that bedroom."

"So, you were in that bedroom and then you shot Mr. Hamilton?"

His eyes caught her assumption. "No, that's not what I'm saying. Listen, everyone, let me start at the beginning. After Poppy told me she was going to be spending more time with Mr. Hamilton again that weekend, I got really upset. After we argued and she left, I got to drinking. I then drove to the Hamilton's to give both of them a piece of my mind. But I wasn't as drunk as usual, so I actually thought it through. I decided I would go in through that side bedroom window and spy on them. I wanted to see if I would catch them red-handed in any kind of romantic way. I took my screwdriver and pried the window open and climbed in. I slowly started towards the door to carefully open it, when I heard a voice—it was Poppy's. I started to peek through the door jamb when someone suddenly walked past the door, so I slowly closed it back up. That's probably the door that Poppy heard closing. I lost my nerve about confronting them, so I quickly went back out the window and then began walking back to my truck. About the time I was opening the door to my truck, I heard the gunshot. I closed the door to my truck, and that's when May and Darlene say they saw me. Then I made my way through the front door and over to where all of you were standing in the study. And I'm telling the truth, that's how it happened."

"That's how '*he claims*' it happened," said Daniel. "He could be making up that story to cover his crime."

Eve added. "Aren't we also forgetting about the gun? Sergeant McMurphy stated the gun in Ralph's glove compartment was just recently fired. And it was a .38, the same type of gun that shot my husband. He claims he shot in the air to scare some kids at his house, but how do we know he's telling the truth? And even if he did shoot the gun to scare those kids, that doesn't mean he didn't shoot my husband also. I've seen him come over here drunk so many times, that I don't believe a word he says anymore."

Steele cleared his throat. "Alright, if nobody has any other evidence or anything further to add, then maybe we should take a vote. First of all, let's vote on Daniel. Do we believe he was in fact in the bathroom the whole time? And take into consideration that he did have time to shoot Mr. Hamilton and then rush back into the bathroom before Poppy turned the corner of the hallway to spot him. And I know it was probably the jewelry box in his front pocket coming out of Hanover's, but that doesn't mean he didn't buy a gun some other time."

Darlene raised her hand. "I'm not saying this because he's my brother, but like Poppy, I also smelled something bad when we walked past that bathroom. A smell like that you cannot fake."

May added. "I didn't want to say anything either for Daniel's sake, but I smelled it also. And it was more than just flatulence."

Steele pointed down the hallway. "Before we vote, why don't all of us go into the study instead of being scattered throughout this hallway."

Everyone filtered into the study, as Steele gathered their attention. "Alright, all of you who feel Daniel committed this crime, raise your hands."

No one raised their hands to convict Daniel Thomas except Ralph Sorenson. However, Steele noticed that Poppy started to raise her hand, but then lowered it and folded her arms.

He turned to her. "Poppy? You started to raise your hand, then lowered it. What is your vote?"

Tears began to pool in her eyes. "You're making me vote to acquit Daniel, but in reality, it's a vote against my husband. And what we're voting on could send a person to jail for the rest of their lives. But even so, let me tell you why I hesitate to vote. When my husband looked into my eyes and said he was telling the truth, I saw a look I had never seen before. It was a look of desperation and hope. He had a look of desperation because he knew this was his last chance to convince people he was innocent. But he also had hope in his eyes, and that hope was in me. For me to believe in him no matter what happened. It's for this reason I cannot place a vote for either of these men. I think it's only right that a woman stands by her man if she believes he's telling the truth."

Ralph looked caringly into Poppy's eyes and mouthed the words, I love you, as she did the same.

Sergeant McMurphy cleared his throat. "Okay, but in law, we have to go by the majority. And, with the majority acquitting Daniel of this crime, I would say we move to a vote on Ralph Sorenson. Again, this is just an informal vote for this reenactment. He will have his day in court if formal charges are brought against him."

Steele nodded his head in agreement. "Thank you, Sergeant; I feel we should proceed as you suggest." He scanned the group. "Everyone in favor of accusing Ralph Sorenson of this crime, raise your hands."

All hands were raised, except for Poppy; with Steele reluctantly raising his hand also.

"Alright," said Sergeant McMurphy. "It appears the majority has decided that we should follow through on charges against Ralph Sorenson in the shooting of Mr. Randall Hamilton."

Poppy moved in front of the group. "Please, I know he has anger issues and has not told the truth many times. But I just know in my heart he did not do this." She turned to Steele. "Please, there has to be another explanation—another suspect."

Steele laid a consoling hand on her shoulder. "I am so sorry, Poppy, but without any other evidence, we have to go with what we have. And right now, we have your husband having the means. He admitted he was in that bedroom at the time of the shooting. Also, the evidence. He owns a .38 pistol in his glove compartment which had just been fired. And a motive. His motive to do bodily harm to Mr. Hamilton is because he felt he was having an affair with you. I'm afraid with this evidence, we will have to proceed with criminal prosecution for attempted murder. I'm sorry, but there is nothing we can do."

Poppy burst into tears once more. May walked over and placed a consoling arm around her.

Eve Hamilton then tucked her purse under her arm. "If there isn't anything further, Mr. Steele, are we free to go?"

Steele glanced around at all the faces in the room. That famous gut of his was telling him they were missing something. Something just didn't add up, but he couldn't place his finger on it.

He replied, "No, I guess there isn't anything else. But hold on for a minute, Eve, I want to talk to you before you go."

She nodded her head. "That's fine."

As the rest of the group began to gather their things, the phone rang. Sergeant McMurphy answered it and listened for a few moments.

He quickly motioned to Steele. "It's that call you've been waiting for."

Steele walked over and began to talk to the man on the phone. Suddenly his eyes grew wide and he covered the phone with his hand. "Wait, everyone! No one leave yet."

Steele went back to the phone and listened intently to what he was being told. After he hung up the phone, he walked over to Kit and pulled her aside.

"Kit, what I was told on that phone may just break this case wide open. I'll explain later, but I'm going to need you, so just follow my lead."

She nodded her head. "I got it. By the look in your eyes, you must have gotten some very interesting information from that call."

He directed a look of uncertainty. "Well, we'll see in a few minutes."

Steele gathered everyone's attention. "Ladies and gentlemen, some new evidence has just been brought to my attention that may well have a bearing upon this reenactment."

"Don't we already have the right person," Daniel asked, in a wearied voice.

"Please everyone, with this new information you will be seeing this investigation unfold as I try to put the pieces together. I know you all are curious, but soon you will understand."

Steele motioned to Sergeant McMurphy. "I'm going to need your help in a minute."

"No problem, but what about our suspect, Ralph Sorenson?"

"I'm not sure how all of this is going to play out, so if you can, cuff him to something secure so he can't try to escape."

Sergeant McMurphy directed to Steele a questioning stare. "Alright, I hope you know what you're doing."

Steele raised his brow. "I hope so too."

As everyone in the room watched, Steele turned to one of the deputies. "Find me something to stand on so I can look on top of one of these bookcases."

The deputy walked over to one of the French Regency mahogany chairs and leaned down to pick it up.

Steele shouted, "No! don't touch those chairs! Out of respect for Mr. Hamilton, I know he doesn't want those chairs moved."

Steele's eyes sharpened as his mind swirled upon hearing his own words. Those were the same words that Mr. Hamilton had spoken to him right before he lost consciousness.

Steele also recalled his conversation with May about the chairs being moved. She had commented how Mr. Hamilton noted that recently one of the chairs had been moved and it seemed to bother him very much.

Steele turned to the deputy. "Find something else to stand on. There must be a stepping stool or something nearby."

The deputy found a stepladder laying on the far side of one of the bookcases. There were five bookcases in all which lined the back wall. Steele took the stepladder and made a beeline for the fourth bookcase towards the right side of the room. Each of the five bookcases had two evenly spaced ceramic figures on top of each one. On top of this particular bookcase, were eagle figures. He stepped on the ladder and then took the ceramic eagle off the left-hand side, turned it over, and took a plastic plug out of the bottom. He jiggled the ceramic eagle and something fell in his hand—it was a key! He turned and showed the key to everyone in the room, as their eyes grew wide with interest. He moved his hand along the back edge when he felt something touch his finger.

He turned to Sergeant McMurphy. "You may want to come closer. I want you to be next to me once I place this key inside the keyhole."

Sergeant McMurphy stood next to the stepladder, as Steele placed the key into the slot and turned it. Suddenly, there was a click of a lock opening, and the bookcase to the left of him slightly opened. Everyone's eyes were filled with surprise and amazement.

"What is that?" said Kit. "Is there something behind there?"

Steele stepped down from the ladder and turned to address the group. "I got a call from a Mr. Brown who is a close friend of Mr. Hamilton. He told me that Mr. Hamilton showed him a secret hidden room behind the bookcases. In it, were other valuable items to his collection; including more guns. He told me exactly how to open the bookcase to unlock this hidden room."

Everyone in the room looked at each other with wonder, as Steele instructed the deputy to open the bookcase further. As it began to open, different items began to reveal themselves in the darkness of the room. First some paintings on the walls, and then a display full of rare coins. Steele then drifted over to a glass display case, which was filled with more vintage guns.

He motioned to Sergeant McMurphy. "We need to make sure nobody touches anything in here. There may be fingerprints or evidence we don't know about."

Sergeant McMurphy turned to the group. "Alright, please stay where you are. It's fine to look, but we need to keep this area secure."

Eve Hamilton moved forward. "I cannot believe this. So, this is where that man has been keeping his other valuables." She shook her head. "I still don't know why he couldn't have told me about this room. It's not like I care so much about his silly collections."

Steele looked closer into the gun case and pointed to a particular weapon. "There is a gun here that is labeled, Smith & Wesson .38 Special circa 1900."

The date of being a turn of the century gun hung in the air like a balloon ready to pop—then it did, in Steele's memory.

Sergeant McMurphy pointed to the side of the display. "The lock on this case is open. It doesn't make sense that Mr. Hamilton would leave this open with all these valuable guns."

Eve exhaled a breath filled with annoyance. "Typical. He probably took one of the guns out of the case to show to his former college buddies. He must have forgotten to lock it because he was too busy acting like a bigshot."

Ralph Sorenson shouted from being handcuffed to a radiator. "Hey! maybe one of the guns in that case is the one that shot Mr. Hamilton."

Steele and Sergeant McMurphy looked at one another with a questioning stare. Sergeant McMurphy then opened the lid to the display, as Steele took his handkerchief from his shirt pocket and took hold of the Smith & Wesson .38 Special as to not place any prints on it. He lifted it to his nose and smelled the barrel. He then allowed Sergeant McMurphy to smell the barrel also. They nodded in agreement.

Steele then walked over in front of the group. "This gun has been recently fired."

A gasp went up amongst the group, as they all began to look at each other with suspicion.

Steele had Sergeant McMurphy dust the gun for prints. When he was done, he shook his head in the negative.

Steele stood in deep thought as he attempted to make sense of the evidence which was unfolding. He walked over to May Wilson and pulled her to the side.

"May, I need your help. Please, put your personal feelings aside for the sake of this investigation. I have a hunch where this is all leading, but I need something from you."

May looked into Steele's eyes which were filled with desperation.

"Alright," she said. "For the sake of the investigation."

Steele spoke in a hushed tone. After he asked his question, May glanced to the side in deep thought. Then she leaned in and whispered her response. As her words caught Steele's ears, his eyes narrowed in acknowledgment of what was said.

He looked into her eyes. "Thank you, May; thank you so much."

Steele began to walk back in front of the group when Poppy pulled him to the side.

"When I saw May whisper something to you, I realized there was something else I had not told you."

Poppy pulled Steele even further away so no one could hear her. She whispered the information, which was a bit lengthy. When she was done, Steele nodded his head in acknowledgment.

"Thank you, Poppy. You may not know it, but what you and May have told me are two key elements I need to solve this case. Now, if I can only obtain the physical evidence."

Steele returned and motioned to Kit and Sergeant McMurphy. "I want both of you to come with me. I need your help searching for some clues and also for you to be witnesses if we find something."

Sergeant McMurphy told his deputies to make sure no one left the room, unless for a bathroom emergency.

As they began to leave the room, Daniel spoke up. "Where are you three going? First, you have all this secretive whispering, and now your off to do something else. This is getting ridiculous! I'm just getting over my food poisoning, but I'm still feeling weak. How much more of this do we have to go through? Besides, you already have the person who did it; he's cuffed to that radiator."

Steele turned to the group. "Listen everyone; in light of finding this hidden room, and now other testimony, we have to investigate a little further. Hopefully, it won't be too much longer. If some of you like, one of the deputies can escort you into the living room to sit on the furniture. Then when we are ready, we will gather back in this study."

Everyone went to the living room and took a seat on the furniture. Steele, Kit and Sergeant McMurphy walked through the house and over to the furthest hallway and towards the door that led into the back patio. They walked into the patio as Steele looked around the room.

"Alright, now based on Poppy's new testimony, I feel we need to look for new clues in this area. There has to be something here to make sense of her statement."

Sergeant McMurphy then moved a large empty box that was blocking some kind of door.

He motioned to Steele. "Do you think what you're looking for could be in this utility room?"

Steele casually walked over, when something caught his attention. He bent down and looked closer at the lock.

Suddenly a look of recollection rose on his face. "This is a Corbin Mortise lock!" He turned to Kit. "I believe this is the same type of lock which the locksmith said a woman had gone into his shop and wanted a key made."

Kit nodded her head. "You're right; I remember the name."

"Why is this important?" asked Sergeant McMurphy.

"Because as Kit and I were following leads, I tracked down a locksmith regarding a woman who might have approached him. The key which this woman had made was to a Corbin Mortise lock."

"And why is this an important clue?"

"Because either May Wilson or Eve Hamilton had access to Mr. Hamilton's keys."

A look of skepticism rose on his face. "And again, how is this going to help solve this case?"

"If we can find the key here on the grounds, that will prove that one of them had a key made. And based on what Poppy told me, it might link to Eve."

Sergeant McMurphy narrowed his brow. "I still don't see why Mrs. Hamilton making a key to a utility door would have anything to do with this investigation. So, she had a key made; people have keys made all the time. I mean, *this is* her house."

"You're right, Sergeant, but it's the timing of all of this that has me questioning a theory I have."

Kit interjected. "When you were talking to the group, I happened to look at Eve. She had this far-off look in her eyes. It was almost like she knew something about the hidden room, but didn't want to speak up." Kit added. "Maybe it's one of those love triangle things. Maybe she has been accusing her husband of having an affair, but in reality, *it's her* who is having an affair. And maybe she is having an affair with one of her husband's college buddies. Then that man decided to get rid of Mr. Hamilton so he could have Eve to himself."

Steele glanced to the side. "Hmm, I never thought of that. But that actually could go along with what May Wilson just got through telling me. May told me that the revised Will said, that upon Mr. Hamilton's death, that Eve would now get half of *everything*. Including his business assets and property, which is a lot of money. If you remember, Eve was only going to get half of what Mr. Hamilton earned during their three-year marriage. But for some reason, he changed it. And since I suspect that Eve got a look at the Will, she might have told one of his college buddies of the change to the Will. And in turn, maybe this man tried to kill Mr. Hamilton." Steele glanced out the corner of his eye. "But that doesn't explain how this man could have gotten in and out of the hidden room. It's one thing if he were to hide in there on the day of the shooting. However, Sergeant McMurphy had his officers guarding the house all week long, especially the study, so no one would alter the crime scene. And of course, when we opened the bookcase today, no one was in there."

Kit interjected. "Maybe Eve went back in there somehow and snuck that man out of that room. I mean she has keys to everything in this house. Speaking of keys; what about her purse? Maybe the key to that utility room is still in her purse."

Steele frowned. "No, I checked her purse, remember? I checked it at the time I checked everyone's purses and packages. All that was in there were her car keys, which I knew every one of them from traveling with her for hours. Also, she had a few makeup items and a note of instructions about the hotel. Also, a pair of driving gloves and a small bottle of perfume."

Sergeant McMurphy huffed a breath of impatience. "Mr. Steele, can we move on with this? You said you needed my help investigating something that was said to you."

"Yes, you are right. When I spoke to Poppy right now, she told me that on the day of the shooting, she forgot to mention something. She said when she went to use the bathroom, that she saw Eve Hamilton coming into the back patio through the outside door. My question is... if Eve Hamilton was supposed to be gathering the purses, why was she coming into the back patio from the outside?" Steele gathered his thoughts. "My theory is, that for some reason Eve wanted to get rid of the key. And that's why she volunteered to gather the pursues when Poppy saw her coming into the patio."

Sergeant McMurphy shrugged his shoulders. "Okay, let's have a look outside for this alleged key. But I still don't know what this has to do with finding evidence as to who shot Mr. Hamilton."

Steele held that thin-lipped smile of his. "Patience, Sergeant; let's just play this out."

The three of them walked outside the back patio door and began to look around. They looked in several flower pots which lined the base of the patio. Sergeant McMurphy looked at the edges of the windowsills, and Kit looked for disturbed dirt around the plants.

Kit then began to walk towards a water feature in the lawn area, when Steele called her back.

"Not that far off, Kit. If she hid a key, she would have placed it closer. She didn't have much time, so she would have ditched it fast."

As Steele and Sergeant McMurphy continued the search, Kit began to walk back on the stone pavers as to not damage the pristine lawn which was meticulously manicured. She playfully balanced herself on one foot in the middle of each paver, then moved on to the next. As she balanced herself on the third paver, closest to the door, the paver slightly rocked in place. As she looked down at the paver, Steele happened to be looking her way. As their eyes met, they looked at each other in acknowledgment of what the other was thinking. Kit moved her foot off the paver as Steele walked over and stood next to her. He reached down and turned over the stone paver, and lo and behold, there was the key!

Steele bent down and was about to grab the key when Sergeant McMurphy took hold of his arm.

"Don't touch it; use my handkerchief; I don't want your prints on it—we want to preserve evidence. I have my fingerprint kit here with me, so we can dust it for prints."

Steele took the handkerchief, picked up the key, and looked it over carefully. "It definitely looks like a key that would go into that Corbin Mortise deadbolt lock. And guess what? It's a brand-new key just recently made. This would go along with what we suspected; that Eve had this key made for some reason at the locksmith shop."

Steele looked towards the utility room door. "Let's try this key in that door lock and maybe there will be some evidence of what we are looking for. Remember, I'm just trying to figure this out as we go along."

Steele took hold of the key which was still partially wrapped in the handkerchief. He slowly placed it inside and turned the key, when he heard the click of the deadbolt. The three of them looked at each other in anticipation of what they would find behind the door.

Steele opened the door fully so that both Sergeant McMurphy and Kit could see inside. As the three of them peered inside, each one seemed to be frozen in awe. Slowly, they glanced at one another with growing amazement rising on their faces.

Steele turned to Sergeant McMurphy. "We'll head back to the study and gather everyone together. This next part of this investigation is going to be very interesting."

He turned to Kit and gave her some instructions on what to do.

"I got it," said Kit. "Just give me the word, and I'll see you over there."

Chapter Twelve

Steele and Sergeant McMurphy dusted the key for prints before making their way to the living room. Once again, no prints were found on the key, as it appeared to be wiped clean. One of the deputies met them in the hallway and told Sergeant McMurphy he had a phone call. After he got off the phone, he told Steele what was said. Based upon what he was told, Steele then instructed Sergeant McMurphy as to what his plan of action was going to be. They walked into the living room and told everyone to follow them back into the study. As everyone filtered into the room, Steele gathered their attention.

"Ladies and gentlemen, there have been a few new developments. Some of these developments we still need to play out, but by the time we are done, you will know the person that attempted to kill Mr. Hamilton."

Daniel huffed a breath of impatience. "I feel as if we are riding on top of a broken record. This whole thing keeps going around and around, over and over." He pointed to Ralph Sorenson. "Don't we have the right person already in cuffs?"

Steele cleared his throat. "Listen, I know we are all tired, but please just hear me out as I begin to explain this whole thing."

Eve interjected. "Let Mr. Steele finish his investigation. All of this is still part of the original case I hired him for, so let's hear him out."

Steele nodded in appreciation. "Thank you, Eve."

He turned to the group. "Now before I disclose the perpetrator, let me go back a bit. After I got a call from one of Mr. Hamilton's college buddies, he told me about the hidden room.

As Sergeant McMurphy and I investigated the room, we found a gun; a .38 revolver that had recently been fired. We dusted it for prints at that time, but we found nothing. We also found something else, which was very interesting. On the furthest bookcase on our right, on the third shelf from the top, there was a sliding panel about four inches by six inches. Meaning, it was there so the person in the hidden room could see into the study. In our minds, this opened up the possibility there was someone in the hidden room who loaded that .38 from the display case, and in turn, shot Mr. Hamilton through that sliding panel."

Everyone looked around with confusion on their faces.

Poppy raised her hand with the obvious question. "Mr. Steele, if someone was in that hidden room, and all the rest of us were somewhere else in the house, then none of us in this room could have possibly shot Mr. Hamilton."

Steele countered, "Not exactly. *There was* someone in that hidden room, and that person *did shoot* Mr. Hamilton."

May interjected. "How is that possible? There is only one way in and out of that hidden room, and that's through the bookcase door."

"Actually, that's not true," he said.

He then prompted everyone to move in closer so they could see inside the hidden room.

Steele then turned and shouted in a loud voice. "Okay Kit, come on in!"

Everyone turned and looked to the front door of the study waiting for Kit to walk in. Instead, a strange sound was heard near the wall in the back corner of the hidden room. Suddenly, a secret door popped open! Kit brushed through the opening and stood in the room. Everyone's mouths dropped wide open.

Poppy moved forward and peered into the secret passageway. "Where does this corridor go to?"

"It goes all the way into what is labeled the utility room in the back patio."

Eve shook her head. "My husband and his secrets. He must have had this secret passageway placed into the house at the time he had this house built."

Poppy interjected. "I still don't know how the perpetrator could be one of us? Like May pointed out, all of us were account-ed for at the time the lights went out and Mr. Hamilton was shot."

"Not exactly," said Steele. "Now this may take a bit of explain-ing, but let me start by giving a rundown of all the suspects in this room."

As Steele stood in front of the group, the anticipation of the moment was thicker than molasses. Each one began to look at the other with suspicion.

Steele then walked and stood in front of May Wilson. The group looked at May in disbelief.

"Little May Wilson; she appears to be as innocent as Rebecca of Sunnybrook Farm; or is she? Because of work related activi-ties, May has been at this Southport house many times. Because of this, May could have figured out how to get into the hidden room. Or perhaps because Mr. Hamilton trusted her so much, he might have even told her about it. May also works side by side with Mr. Hamilton at his office, so she would have had opportu-nities at the office to duplicate a particular key of his. I won't say any more about this key at this time, but very soon you will un-derstand why I brought up the subject of the key. Now, you might ask what was her motive? Her motive, like so many in this life, could have been money. When I was short on a motive for May being involved in this, I did a little digging. In fact, no one knew I did this research," he said and turned to Kit with an apologetic stare. "In a conversation, May had told me she met Darlene at the courthouse dealing with a personal matter. Court matters that are adjudicated are public record so I did some searching through those records. I found out that May owes a bail bondsman a lot of money because she posted bail for an uncle of hers who got arrested for a serious crime. However, after the bail was posted, this uncle fled the state and never returned to be tried. You might say he left May holding the bag, and now May has to pay off this bail bond by making monthly payments on a three-thousand-dollar bond. Another reason why May might have been involved in this conspiracy, is that May is a woman who has high career aspirations for her life. And usually, to achieve those aspirations you need money. Now, May being Mr. Hamilton's secretary had access to his Will. I also saw a book on her desk about being a contract lawyer. In this book, I'm sure it mentions contracts such as setting up a Will. She would then know which beneficiary page she would need to alter to make herself listed as receiving a portion of that Will and no one would be the wiser if Mr. Hamilton was dead."

May looked into Steele's eyes with disappointment and hurt at Steele's accusations. Tears began to well in her eyes, but she said nothing in her defense.

Seeing the tears welling in her eyes caused Steele to swallow hard as his emotions ran deep. But he had to be impartial—he had a job to do.

He then walked over to the next person who was Darlene Thomas.

"Let me tell you what Darlene's motive could have been to commit this crime. Darlene cares very much about her brother. When I first met Darlene, it was easy to draw out her anger towards Mr. Hamilton because she cares so much for her brother. It hurt her to see him fall to the depths like he did, so she understandably had resentment towards him. This opens up the possibility that this resentment played a part in her wanting to get back at Mr. Hamilton. In regards to her part in this, Darlene is good friends with May and could have influenced May in this conspiracy against Mr. Hamilton because she knew May needed the money. Knowledge of this conspiracy started when Darlene and May met at the Lakeside Country Club. Darlene was given an envelope of money from May to purchase a gun, which was witnessed by my assistant Kit. And as I said before, May and Darlene are each other's alibi, so of course they would lie to cover each other. One of them could have slipped out of that entertainment room and went into the back patio, through the utility door, and into the hidden room and shot Mr. Hamilton. May or Darlene could have stayed hidden in the passageway until Eve switched the power back on and left that area to check on her husband. And if you remember, Eve said she could not see into all areas of the entertainment room to verify if both of them were actually in the room."

Darlene directed to Steele a look of disbelief. "I swear to you, I was not involved in any conspiracy to kill Mr. Hamilton."

May then placed a consoling hand on her shoulder and said, everything would be alright.

Steele then stood in front of Daniel. "You know Daniel, there is a saying from the play, Hamlet. It is in reference to someone who protests so much that they are no longer believable. The saying is, 'the lady doth protest too much', or in your case, the man doth protest too much."

A look of shock rose upon his face. "Me? I didn't do this!"

"Daniel, of everyone here you have the biggest motive because of what Mr. Hamilton did to you and your business. As I stated earlier, in connection with Darlene and May, you could have played a part in this conspiracy to kill Mr. Hamilton by purchasing the gun. I mean, how sweet that would be to see Mr. Hamilton dead for what he did to you and at the same time, get a lot of money out of it. The three of you could have agreed to divvy up the monies from the Will. However, I will say you couldn't have been the one who pulled the trigger. Since Poppy heard and smelled you in the bathroom at the time of the shooting, that gets you off of attempted murder. However, that doesn't get you off as a co-conspirator along with May and Darlene."

Daniel raised his voice. "Are you crazy! May, Darlene and I did not have some conspiracy to kill him!"

Steele then walked over to Ralph Sorenson who was still in cuffs and stood before him.

"For now, Mr. Sorenson, you will remain in cuffs. The evidence against you is substantial, but I'm starting to question if you could have done it—you didn't have access to the key."

The group help pondering stares as they didn't quite understand what he meant by that statement about the key. Steele then walked over and stood before Eve Hamilton, and held that famous thin-lipped smile of his.

"That only leaves one more person to address in this room; Mrs. Hamilton herself. But to explain this fully and cover all aspects of the evidence, I need to go back to the beginning. As I said before, my involvement started when Eve Hamilton hired me to investigate her husband. In the course of our investigation, a few other things surfaced as we thought that May, Darlene, and or Daniel approached a man named Greenie who lived at The Alley, a place where homeless people live. Greenie was known to have information on vendors where you might be able to buy a gun 'under the table.' When I approached Greenie, he told me that two people approached him; a man and a woman. And the man who asked Greenie about purchasing a gun matched Daniel's description. We have since verified that Daniel did in fact go to Hanover's and purchased a vintage gun. However, we do not know if he purchased another gun—a .38. Greenie also said a woman approached him. She was dressed in an overcoat, a bandana covering her head, and rounded sunglasses which pretty much disguised her identity. He said this woman asked where to obtain bullets for a .38. She also asked him if all .38 bullets were the same and would work on a turn of the century model. At the time, the fact that this woman asked about bullets for a .38 did not have any significance until Mr. Hamilton was also shot with a .38. And now considering we found a .38 recently fired in the hidden room, it has *a lot* more significance. Greenie also said this woman asked where to find a safecracker. As mentioned earlier,

I suspected it could have been May Wilson, as she might have needed a safecracker to get into Mr. Hamilton's safe to change out the Beneficiary page of the Will. However, I also thought it could have been Eve Hamilton. The safecracker which Greenie suggested was a man named Denny. Denny is a con-man who is known to deal in under-the-table activities. When I spoke to this Denny, he described the woman he spoke to as having long shapely legs. I suspected that Eve might have needed a safecracker to get into her husband's office safe to look at his Will. It is still unclear as to whether Eve Hamilton actually had a safecracker open the safe, but she had the opportunity. May stated that Eve Hamilton and a man, who was dressed as a janitor, were in Mr. Hamilton's office with the door closed for enough time to get into the safe and look at the Will."

Eve interrupted. "Mr. Steele, I did not have a man *'dressed like a janitor'* break into my husband's safe. *He was* a janitor from another company hired to clean the office and nothing more. Besides, even if I had done those things, what bearing does my wanting to get a look at my husband's Will have on this investigation?"

"Eve, I'm just laying out the foreground of the different angles I was taking as I moved forward in the investigation."

Eve crossed her arms in a defensive posture. "Very well, Mr. Steele, continue. But I don't like my name being mentioned so much in your little scenario."

Steele returned his focus to the group. "As I was saying, the reason why I wanted to find out which one of these women it might be, was to connect other evidence Kit and I discovered in the investigation. Now, when I went to these vendors and asked for a description of the woman, they told me the same description as Greenie did. So based on that fact, I did not know for sure who the woman was, but I had my suspicions."

May interjected. "So that's why you came into the office again and commented on my bandana? You suspected that I was that woman?"

"Yes, May, as I said before, I had a job to do and I had to keep an open mind on all suspects."

Steele turned back to the group. "Now, let's move forward to the evening where Mr. Hamilton was shot. Because I didn't know who might be a suspect, I told everyone to stay in the study. I also wanted to look at any evidence that was brought into the house. I told Poppy to go gather the women's purses and the gift boxes from the entertainment room. However, Eve volunteered instead; saying it was too hard to see her husband lying on the floor. Eve then walked out the door to gather those belongings. However, tonight when I spoke to Poppy, she reminded me that when Eve left the room to get the purses, that she and Daniel requested to go to the bathroom. Since Daniel rushed into the bathroom in the nearest hallway, Poppy then had to go to the one in the hallway where the entertainment room is located. This is where Poppy saw something that caught her attention. She saw Eve Hamilton coming in from the outside and into the back patio. When Poppy told me this, things began to click in my head."

Eve interrupted. "First of all, I don't see that my being in any location in *my own house* is anyone's business," she said and glared at Poppy. "But if you must know, I have a reason for being outside."

Eve glanced to the side, took a breath, then returned her focus. "I went out the back patio door because I saw my neighbors' dog in the yard. The dog has done this before and he 'messes' on our perfectly manicured lawns. Therefore, I shooed him away, and that is why Poppy saw me coming in through that back door."

Steele walked and stood in front of Eve with that famous thin-lipped smile of his.

He then turned to the group, as the tone in his voice changed; indicating he was ready to bring the hammer down on the perpetrator.

He pointed to Ralph Sorenson. "Sergeant McMurphy, please uncuff Mr. Sorenson. I know for a fact he did not commit this crime."

Daniel began to protest when Steele stopped him. "Everyone, please hold your judgments and opinions until I'm done explaining all of this. After I am finished you will understand."

Sergeant McMurphy uncuffed Ralph Sorenson as Poppy walked over to be by his side.

Chapter Thirteen

S teele cleared his throat to gather everyone's attention. "And now we come to the final chapter of this; and to the only person I have yet to fully address—Eve Hamilton. Eve, a person who out of all of you, had a solid steel alibi. After all, she is the one who hired me in the first place. She was also by my side practically the whole time this crime was committed. Now Kit came up with an interesting theory. She thought that perhaps Eve was deflecting her own guilt of having an affair, by accusing her husband of the same. Kit thought the man whom Eve might be having an affair with, was one of Mr. Hamilton's former college buddies. And in turn, this man wanted Eve to himself so he was the one who shot Mr. Hamilton. However, just before we started, Sergeant McMurphy got another telephone call. It was from the other two college buddies of Mr. Hamilton. These two men are at a symposium in Greece and have been there for two weeks. And since the other man has been out of the country in Canada, none of these three men could have possibly attempted to kill Mr. Hamilton. So, after putting all the pieces together, I can only conclude the guilty person is... Eve Hamilton!"

A look of shock rose on everyone's face.

Eve placed her hands on her hips. "I beg your pardon! What are you accusing me of, Mr. Steele? You yourself said I have a solid steel alibi."

"Let me continue, Mrs. Hamilton."

"Very well, but let me just say here and now; you are fired!"

Steele turned back to address the group. "After Poppy told me about Eve being outside, I found it odd because she should have just walked straight into the entertainment room to pick up the purses and gift boxes, then walked back out. And despite her little story about the dog messing on the lawn, I realized that Eve has been lying all along. When Eve and I were trying to catch Mr. Hamilton and Poppy having an affair, I was outside the study at the French doors, and Eve was to go through the front door and wait under the stairwell. But now I know that's not what she did. She rushed around the side of the house, into the backyard, and went into the back patio. From there she used the key she had made from the locksmith at Henry's, to open the utility room door which leads to the passageway and into the hidden room. She had to have a key made because Mr. Hamilton had the only key to that utility door. Since you can hear pretty well through that passageway and into the hidden room adjacent to the study, Eve waited until the top of the hour at six o'clock when the grandfather clock began to chime. She then turned off the lights on the electric panel and rushed through the passageway. She did this because she knew Poppy would then leave the study and head to turn the lights back on, as she wanted no witnesses. She had previously loaded the gun from the display case in the hidden room with the bullets she had bought at a gun shop. The same caliber bullets to which she had asked Greenie if new .38 bullets would work on a turn of the century model gun. And as we know, the gun in the display case is a turn-of-the-century model dating back to 1900. Then as Poppy left the room to head to turn the power back on, Eve quietly moved that sliding panel to the side and she shot her husband. Eve then quickly placed the gun back in the case, but it didn't fully lock because she was in such a hurry to get back out through the passageway and into the back patio. When Poppy heard the gunshot and was about to head back to the study, she heard a door close. That's when she went back through the kitchen and into the hallway to see what that sound was and saw Eve near the back door. But instead of Eve's story of being near the back door to turn the lights back on, Eve was actually just getting back into the back patio through the passageway. Now, at this point, I am sure you are all wondering what Eve's motive would have been to kill her husband. After all, wasn't she trying to gather evidence to divorce him? Well, to give you the short answer; it was greed. You see, a while ago I pulled May aside and asked her a question. I asked her what was the change in the revised Will. She told me there was no change in the event of their divorce. However, *there was a change* in the amount Eve Hamilton would receive upon his death. You see, the original Will said that Eve would get half of what they earned together only during their marriage; which isn't that much. However, Mr. Hamilton changed the Will and now Eve would get half of *everything*, including his business assets and financial portfolio which is worth millions. In other words, Eve now knew that her husband was worth more dead than alive."

As Steele continued, suspicious eyes began to drift over to Eve.

"Now, this takes me to the part about the key. I had Kit and Sergeant McMurphy go with me to investigate why Eve had gone outside when she was supposed to be gathering the purses. As we looked around in the patio, we found a door that said, Utility Room. I then remembered the locksmith had told me that the woman wanted a key made was for a Corbin Mortise deadbolt lock. Well, guess what... that utility room door has a Corbin Mortise deadbolt lock on it. Then Kit and I got to thinking. If Eve Hamilton had that key made, she wouldn't have wanted me to find it when I searched through the purses. She would have needed to get rid of the key and hide it. And that's why we figured Eve volunteered to gather the purses to give her time to hide the key. As the three of us went outside and began looking for this key, Kit happened to step foot on a stone paver that wobbled ever so slightly. I overturned the stone paver and sure enough, there was the key. I walked over to the utility room door and it opened the lock. I opened the door thinking perhaps there was a heating unit or water heater, but instead, we saw a passageway. A passageway we knew went into that hidden room behind the bookcase. We gathered all of you together in that room, and that's when you saw Kit come from out of that passageway through a hidden panel."

Eve interrupted. "Mr. Steele, what makes you think that I was the one who placed that key under that stone paver? As you said earlier, May had access to my husband's keys at the office so she could have made a duplicate. Not to mention, May also had access to my husband's Will. You're also assuming that my husband didn't place a spare key there himself; did you think of that? Or better yet, he's so proud of his gun collection, that he made a spare key so his college buddies could bring their friends to see the guns anytime they like."

Steele held that thin-lipped smile. "I tell you, Mrs. Hamilton, you should be a writer to come up with these explanations on the spot."

Eve added. "What about fingerprints? Shouldn't you check to see if anyone's fingerprints are on that key?"

"We did. Sergeant McMurphy dusted the key for prints, but unfortunately, there were no prints on the key—it was wiped clean."

"Then you see; you have no evidence of my wrongdoing. Accusing me of something like this—this is an outrage!"

"Just wait, Mrs. Hamilton, I'm not done with explaining this investigation, so let me continue. As I was saying, when Kit came through the passageway and into the hidden room, we all knew it was possible for one of us to be the guilty person."

Eve took a step forward. "So, let me get this straight. First, you say it was I who went to this Greenie man and asked him where to find some bullets. Yet this Greenie man could not make a positive identification of the woman he talked to. And as you said yourself, it could have been May who talked to this man. Then you went to some locksmith who could not identify this woman either. You also said you spoke to a safecracker named Denny, where the only identification he gave you, was that the woman had a *nice pair of legs*. And as I am sure you have noticed, all of us women in this room have nice legs. Then you made the point of the bullets being from a .38 gun. Which by the way, has been the most popular model and caliber gun for the past forty years! A gun that has been used by military and police for decades." She turned to Sergeant McMurphy. "Sergeant, what kind of gun do you currently use?"

"I currently use a .45, but both of my deputies carry .38's."

Eve held a proud smile. "So, you see Mr. Steele, the fact that some woman bought bullets for a .38, is like saying that the perpetrator happens to like ice cream."

The group then turned to Steele for his response.

"I see your point, Mrs. Hamilton; however, this same woman had a key made that happens to go to a door lock that matches the door lock to that utility room. And besides, when you put everything together, it all points to you."

"Mr. Steele, I don't think you have anything. You don't live with a man like Randall who lives and breathes the law, without learning a thing or two. All this evidence you say you have is called circumstantial. Without a witness to positively identify me as doing these things you say, there is not a judge or jury who would convict me."

Steele held an inner smile as if holding a trump card. "Actually, you're wrong, *there is someone* who can identify you."

"And who might that be?"

"Your husband!"

"My husband? My husband is lying in a hospital bed and is most likely not going to make it. How can he be the one to make a positive identification that I was the one who did it?"

"Because he told me through his last breath before passing out."

Eve held a questioning stare. "What are you talking about?"

"As I held him in my arms, he said the word, 'chair.' I asked him what about the chair? He then said, 'chair, moved.' Now, most of you may think that was just some random words spoken by a dying man, but they weren't. While I was talking to May Wilson at the office, we got to talking about Mr. Hamilton being obsessed with things being in their proper place. She gave an example that one time she and Mr. Hamilton went into this study. This was on a Friday and no one was supposed to have been in the house all week. When they walked into the study, Mr. Hamilton immediately knew something was off. He walked over and noted that one of the chairs had been moved. He always has those Regency fireside chairs placed in their exact locations, as there are indentation marks in the rug where the feet of the chairs are to be placed. He then commented that this was very odd because Poppy and the cleaning lady know how particular he is about those chairs, and he couldn't understand why that chair was out of place. But you see, in his last breath before he passed out, he was letting me know who shot him. He knew that someone, who has a key to this study, must have gone into the study and used that chair to look on top of the bookcases to try to find a way into the hidden room. So, as it turned out, Mr. Hamilton himself identified the person who shot him. And that person was you!"

Eve held a smirk of a smile. "My husband says some random words and this is proof I tried to kill him? Poppy also has a key to this study so she could be the one he was talking about. Let's not forget, Poppy was the person who was closest to my husband at the time of the shooting. It would have been so easy for her to walk out of the study, grab the gun which she previously placed into one of the vases, then go back in and shoot Randall, then simply place the gun back into the vase and continue walking down the hallway. And remember, there is no proof that the gun in the hidden room is the one that shot Randall. In the back of our property, Randall has his own shooting range where he and his buddies take target practice. How do you know they didn't use that .38 from the display case and that's why the barrel smelled recently fired? I can come up with many scenarios to prove others had motives and means to kill him. Honestly, Mr. Steele, I think you are grasping at straws. And besides, with no fingerprints on that key or the gun from inside the hidden room, you have nothing!"

Steele hated to admit it, but he knew she was right. Unless there was some kind of physical evidence to link her, this was all circumstantial. There had to be something—something he was missing. As he stood thinking, he then recalled Eve's last statement of having no fingerprints on the key or the gun. Suddenly, his eyes twinkled with revelation.

"You know Eve, you are right; this is all circumstantial evidence which might not hold up in court. And let me say, you have been a worthy adversary from the time we first met at my office late that evening. And you had this all planned out, down to the very last detail. Including having an answer for every bit of evidence I accused you of. And to top it off, you had me as your witness—your solid steel alibi. Someone who was an investigator and goes by the law to stand as your witness. Someone who was by your side practically the whole time this crime was being committed. And you are right, there are no fingerprints on the key or the gun from the hidden room. However, there is one thing you forgot about."

Steele turned to Sergeant McMurphy. "Can you get your kit that reveals blowback residue from powder marks?"

"Yes, I have it right here on the credenza." He walked to the credenza and brought it over.

Steele then walked over in front of Eve Hamilton, as she looked at him with a questioning stare.

"More of your games?" she said. "Do you really think you will find gunpowder marks on my hands? In case you have forgotten, the day my husband was shot was a week ago. You don't think the person who did this has already taken a shower, or at the very least, washed their hands?" Eve displayed a proud winning smile. "Once again, you have absolutely no proof."

"The proof is not on your hands; the proof is in your purse. Please hand your purse over to Sergeant McMurphy."

Eve huffed a sarcastic laugh. "What could I have in my purse that could possibly give you the proof you are looking for—the smoking gun?"

Eve handed her purse to Sergeant McMurphy. He opened the purse and Steele looked inside. A little grin lifted the edges of his lips as he slowly began to pull out a set of driving gloves. He held them by the cuff as to not touch the fingers. When Eve saw what he had in his hands, her eyes caught Steele's intent, and suddenly a look of worry drew upon her face.

As everyone in the group began to gather around, Sergeant McMurphy took out his kit and began to delicately dust one of the gloves.

Steele addressed the group. "You see, because Mrs. Hamilton did not want any fingerprints on the gun, she wore gloves. Therefore, if there is gunshot residue on these gloves, a scattering of little black dots will show up all over the gloves."

As Sergeant McMurphy continued, no evidence showed on the first one. However, as he continued the process on the second, which was the right-hand glove, little speckles of tiny black dots began to appear. Soon they practically covered the entire glove.

As the group saw the evidence before them, most raised their eyebrows and a look of shock grew on everyone's face.

Upon seeing the evidence, Eve's face grew to indignance as she directed to Steele a loathing stare.

Finally, after a few moments, she huffed a sigh of surrender. "Fine, Mr. Steele, you have got your man, or should I say, your woman. But you have no idea what it was like to be placed on a spending allowance as if I was some child. This man had so much money he didn't know what to do with it. Yes, he changed his Will to give me more money upon his death. But that still left me with diddly for the coming years of our marriage. I had to make sure his death came sooner than our inevitable divorce. He left me with no other choice."

Steele shook his head. "Left you with no other choice? Eve, don't you think Randall must have truly loved you to change his Will in the first place? You were now going to get half of everything he owned in the event of his death. And as far as your spending allowance, did you even bother to find out why he placed you on an allowance in the first place? If you bothered to find out, you would have discovered that when he was very young his family was very poor. Randall went without food just so his younger brothers and sisters could have something to eat. He decided he would get an education and built his business to be able to have financial security so he and his family, you, would never be poor or hungry again. But after you were married, you began to senselessly burn through money. He was just trying to allow you some time to realize that there are more important things in life than money. Apparently, you never learned that lesson. By changing the Will, he was looking out for your future. Not to mention, that your allowance is more money per week than most people make in a month's salary. Wasn't that enough for you?"

Eve took hold of her purse and tucked it under her arm. "You can never have enough money, Mr. Steele," she said, as a matter of fact.

"No, Mrs. Hamilton, in regards to money, I heard a saying recently from a man I know. This man is not rich, but he is rich in love and happiness. He once told me; if you are not a person of character without having money, then you'll never be a person of character with it."

Sergeant McMurphy began to place the cuffs on Eve. "Mrs. Eve Hamilton, you are under arrest for the attempted murder of your husband Randall Hamilton." As Sergeant McMurphy finished giving Eve her rights and was about to take her off to jail, she turned to Steele one last time.

"You know Mr. Steele; I should have hired Matt Stone after all. He never would have been able to figure out that I was the guilty party. I don't know what went wrong. I had it all figured out down to the very last detail—left no stone unturned."

"You know Mrs. Hamilton, it's ironic how you used that term; left no stone unturned. Because as it turned out, it was when Kit and I 'unturned' that stone paver, that the key to solving this case was revealed. I don't know if you remember, but the night we first met, I said that I'm no choir boy. But since that time, I have learned a few things that Kit has taught me from the good book. There is one scripture that lets us know that even when we think we have left no stone unturned, there is always *someone* who is watching us. That scripture says; if you fail to keep my commandments, you will be sinning against God, and be sure your sin will find you out."

With a look of indifference on her face, Sergeant McMurphy carted Eve Hamilton off in cuffs.

Poppy turned and hugged her husband tight. "Ralph, oh Ralph! I'm so glad you were proven innocent. By the look in your eyes, I just knew you didn't do it."

Ralph hugged her in return. "Thank you for believing in me. I love you so much, Poppy. And from now on, I will learn to trust you and not get jealous."

Kit then walked over and placed a hand on Steele's shoulder. "I see you have been listening when I talk about the Bible. Now if I can just get you to go with me to church service."

Steele warmly cupped her shoulder. "Actually, I think I might just take you up on that this coming Sunday."

Steele then saw May gathering her things to leave, so he quickly walked over and stood before her.

"May, I know you said that I used you; and yes, part of that is true. But please know that I never really thought you to be involved in the attempt on Mr. Hamilton's life. I had to investigate all angles and unfortunately that included looking into you as a suspect. But you can ask Kit; I was defending you all the way."

May looked into his eyes. "As I said before, I understand you had a job to do, but what you did hurt me personally. I am a Christian woman, so we are told to forgive those who have hurt us. However, even though we are to forgive, that doesn't mean we can forget. It may take some time for me to forget this."

Steele nodded his head. "I understand, and I'm so sorry."

Steele continued to get many congratulations from the whole group. As things were wrapping up, Sergeant McMurphy approached him with a firm handshake.

"All I can say is that was incredible how you pieced this all together. As I said before, if you ever want to join our investigative team, I will be more than happy to put in a good word with the commissioner in hiring you."

"Thank you. But for now, I want to keep working on cases independently. But I wouldn't mind working jointly on a case if you should want my assistance."

"I'll remember that, Mr. Steele; I will definitely keep that in mind."

Chapter Fourteen

The following Monday morning, Kit arrived to find Steele looking out the window of his office and down into the street.

"Good morning, Rick. I'm sorry I'm late, but my foster mother wanted to do my hair again. Ever since that time of going to the country club, now she wants to do it all the time. I act like I'm complaining, but I kind of like it. We're getting along pretty good."

"That's great. Don't worry about being late; I just got here myself."

"What were you looking at down in the street?"

"Oh, just Stan the flower man setting things up. He always has such a contented look on his face."

"Well, like you pointed out, he has the right outlook; that life is more than just having worldly possessions."

Steele pulled his attention from the window and turned around. "Yes, I think the Hamilton case has shown me that in ten-fold."

He looked at Kit ready to place her jacket on the coat rack. "Hey, why don't you come with me to breakfast?"

A look of curiosity rose upon her face. "You want me to go with you? You always go alone and then you take donuts over to The Alley."

"I know, but I think a nice little walk and a hearty breakfast will do us some good. Maybe it will clear our minds of all that happened with the Hamilton case. I feel somewhat let down even though we solved the case, as I was disappointed that it ended up being Eve. It's hard to believe that she cared more about money than a human life."

"Yes, I know what you mean."

The two of the closed the office door and walked down the stairs.

Kit added. "Oh, speaking of a human life; any word on Mr. Hamilton's condition?"

"Yes, I wanted to tell you; I got a call from Poppy and she said Mr. Hamilton came out of his comatose state. She said he was talking, and the doctors said it doesn't look like he has any brain damage."

"That's so great! A small miracle."

"Yes, Poppy said Mr. Hamilton was saddened that it was Eve who tried to kill him. However, he said he wasn't that surprised because of the chair being moved—he knew it had to be her. Poppy also told me something which showed the other side of Mr. Hamilton that May was talking about. Poppy told me that Mr. Hamilton said that when he almost died, it made him stop and think about his life. How he has made his business a priority over people and relationships. He then wanted to make amends with people he has hurt, so he placed a call to Daniel Thomas. He offered Daniel a job at the same investment company he has stock in. Daniel is going to be their new Project Manager. It's a very prestigious position where he will be making very good money."

"That's really great. I guess Mr. Hamilton's near-death experience has given him a second chance to do right in his life. Speaking of Mr. Hamilton, did you ever find out why he changed his Will to give Eve half of everything upon his death?"

"Yes, Poppy asked him that very question. The simple answer; was love. Or considering how greedy Eve was; an unconditional love. He told Poppy that even though Eve was selfish, he still wanted to look out for her future. The irony is he was going to take the restriction off her spending. He realized that spending allowance was causing problems between them, so he had decided he was going to lift it."

"Yes, that is pretty ironic. Anything else?"

"Yes. Poppy happened to mention to him about May Wilson owning money on that bail bond. Mr. Hamilton said he would file an action to get the amount reduced or removed entirely."

"Wow, that's so great!"

"And there's more. You're not going to believe what else Poppy told me. She told me that Mr. Hamilton was so grateful for what I did in finding the person who tried to kill him, that he will be sending us a bonus."

"A bonus?"

"Yes, when he found out what Eve did in trying to use me as her alibi, he said I deserved a bonus. He is sending a check for one-thousand dollars."

"One-thousand dollars! Wow, that's a lot of money. Enough money to keep us in business for a lot of years to come."

"Or, we can use some of it for the business and some for college—if you want to go."

Kit narrowed her brow. "Me in college? I had enough problems getting through tenth-grade math."

"Math is just one subject. I believe they have college courses in investigative writing and procedures."

Kit held a pensive stare. "Let me think about it."

As they continued to walk, she added. "Funny how it worked out."

"How is that?"

"Here Eve Hamilton wanted all this money, but in the end, she ended up with nothing."

"Yes, I guess it's like that saying; money can't buy you happiness."

Kit then turned with a questioning stare. "Hey, I forgot to ask you; did you go this morning and try to talk to May Wilson? You said you were going to try one more time to patch things up with her."

Steele held a thin-lipped frown. "Yeah, I did; that's why I was late getting into the office. I even took her a bouquet of flowers I bought from Stan. Unfortunately, she would not accept them. She then seemed to get emotional, so I decided it was best to stop pressuring her. I guess starting up a romance just isn't in the cards for me."

"Well give it some time. Women need time to process and think these things through. Just don't be surprised if one day she happens to walk through your door."

"I kind of doubt it, but thanks for the words of encouragement." Steele then gathered a thought. "Hey, speaking of romances, weren't you supposed to go with Jake to that dance?" He gathered another thought. "Oh no, that was this past Saturday and you were with me in Southport. I made you miss your date with Jake."

Kit shook her head. "No, you didn't make me miss anything. I didn't tell you with all that was going on, but Jake cancelled our date."

"Really? Why?"

"It seems that during the time my foster parents were deciding if they were going to allow me to go or not, Jake got another invitation from this girl Katie. He told me that since I hadn't gotten back to him, he was going to accept her invitation. It kind of surprised me that he suddenly shifted his attention to this other girl so quickly; but no matter, I'm okay with it."

Steele studied her eyes. "Are you sure you're okay with it?"

Kit shrugged her shoulders. "I don't know. I mean, it was going to be my first official date and all, so I'm kind of disappointed because of that."

Steele playfully pulled her to his side. "So much for romances, huh Kit? I guess it's just back to you and me."

She looked up at him and smiled. "Yes, it is, and that's just fine with me."

As they continued to walk, he pointed to the café up ahead. "Let's get some breakfast, deliver some donuts, and then it's on to our next case."

Kit's eyes sparkled with enthusiasm. "Yep, Kit's the name, adventures my game!"

Steele held a wary eye. "Be careful what you wish for. You said that just before the Hamilton case turned into the most difficult case we ever had."

"You're not thinking of going back to cases involving lost cats and dogs, are you?"

Steele laughed. "No, no more cats and dogs."

"That's good; because with the experience we got with the Hamilton case, I think we can handle anything that comes our way."

Steele smiled, as a look of optimism rose upon his face. "So do I, Kit..., so do I."

The End.

I hope you enjoyed the first book of the Richard Steele – Private Eye trilogy.

To continue with the next coming book, look for Richard Steele – Private Eye, (Behind the Steele Curtain.)

To see other books by this author, go to www.fullercreekseries.com and click link to Other Books. All books are available wherever books are sold.

***

Unless otherwise indicated, all scripture references are taken from the Holy Bible, King James Version, Cambridge 1769